Love Lockdown

Also by Mia Edwards

Ghetto Princess

Love Lockdown

Mia Edwards

St. Martin's Griffin
New York

This is a work of fiction. All of the characters, organizations, and events portrayed in this novel are either products of the author's imagination or are used fictitiously.

www.stmartins.com

Library of Congress Cataloging-in-Publication Data

Edwards, Mia.
   Love lockdown / Mia Edwards. — 1st ed.
      p.   cm.
   ISBN 978-0-312-36910-1
  1. African American young women—Fiction.   2. African Americans—Fiction.   3. Drug dealers—Fiction.   4. Revenge—Fiction.   I. Title.
   PS3605.D35L68 2010
   813'.6—dc22

2009039992

First Edition: January 2010

10 9 8 7 6 5 4 3 2 1

Love Lockdown

Chapter 1

always knew I'd have to leave my mama's house, but I never thought it'd be like this," Kanika said as she dumped her last items of clothing into a cardboard box. "I also didn't think I'd be packing all this shit by myself."

"I've been helping you all morning! What you mean?" Sheila asked, and taped up another box.

"*Tyrell.* He should be here." Kanika watched the movers going in and out of the room.

"Admit it, girl—you can't stand being away from him more than a minute. You don't want him wrestling with your boxes, you want him wrestling with you—in the bed."

Kanika blushed. Sheila was right. She needed her man around, but Tyrell was busy getting their travel plans ready.

"You about to be his wife, and you'll never be able to get rid of him," Sheila said. "Just like me and Big Gee. Don't be like us."

Kanika helped Sheila carry the boxes out to the front, where the other ones were. "Tyrell and I have already been apart long enough. I just want to get on that plane already and leave all this craziness behind."

Two years ago she had left Tyrell after finding out that he had slept with her former best friend, Peaches. It had been a one time thing, but it had nearly destroyed her. It had definitely destroyed any trust she had had in Tyrell. Even though she had walked away from him, he wouldn't walk away from her. He had been there during some of the craziest shit in her life. He had calmly walked through fire for her again and again. She sent him away each time, but he would always come back, placing his love and his heart in her hands, until one day it just broke her down. She couldn't send him away again. She had always loved him and she knew she would always love him.

She remembered opening the door to her apartment on her birthday last year. He had two dozen bloodred roses in one hand.

"Tyrell, what are you doing here?" she asked, leaning against the door.

"It's your birthday and I wanted to make sure you was celebrating it right," he told her.

"Thank you, but I'm just going to keep it low-key tonight. Order in and watch some movies, you know? But thanks for stopping by." She started to close the door.

Tyrell put his hand out fast, slapping it angrily against the door. He pushed the door back open and stepped into her hallway. Kanika stared at him as if he was crazy.

"Nigga, what do you think you're doing?"

Tyrell placed the flowers on the table in the entryway and looked at her. His eyes were blazing.

"How long are you going to do this, Kanika?"

"Do what? Get the hell out of my apartment!"

He closed the door behind him. "No, I'm not leaving." He took a step toward her. "How long are you going to keep pushing me away? Don't you know by now I'm not going anywhere without you?"

Kanika put her hands up to her face. "Tyrell, I can't do this right now—"

"That's what you always say."

"And I always mean it!"

He continued to look her dead in her eyes as he came closer and closer. "No, you don't."

Kanika started to back away. "Tyrell—"

He reached out and pulled her to him all of a sudden and kissed her.

Kanika trembled at the feel of Tyrell's lips on hers and moaned when he pushed his tongue into her mouth, tasting her. Her knees almost went weak at the feel of his muscular body pressed up against her small one. Her arms were wedged against his chest as if she were going to push him away, but she couldn't. She couldn't. Oh, God, she had missed him. She had missed him so much. Even on the nights she had cried and cursed his name. Because the truth was that she wished he had never done anything to make him leave her arms.

Tyrell pulled back and looked down at her, his expression tight and almost pained. "Kanika, baby, I'm never going to leave you. You're mine, baby, and I'm yours. And I know I fucked up and hurt you." He swallowed hard. "I know it, Kanika. I live with that shit every time I turn over in bed at night and you're not there. But, baby, that's enough now. You don't have to keep hurting me. I've learned my lesson. I will never, in life, hurt you like that again. So you have to come home now, Kanika. You have to come home now."

Kanika had stared up at him, wanting to believe, wanting to trust, but so afraid. And he must have seen it in her eyes because he bent down and kissed her again. She wrapped her arms around him wanting to swallow him whole. Before she knew it, Tyrell was sweeping her off her feet and carrying her to her bedroom.

He laid her down on the bed, but didn't lie down on top of her right away. Kanika looked up at him questioningly.

"If I get into this bed with you, that's it. You're mine and you're staying mine, Kanika. When it's over, I don't want to hear no shit about me leaving or you leaving." He reached in his pocket and took out a black velvet box. He opened it and showed her what was inside.

"Tyrell!" She gasped. It was a four-carat diamond ring.

"I get in this bed with you and my ring goes on your finger, baby."

Kanika looked up at him feeling like she had been hit by a fucking truck. Was he serious? He wasn't even going to give them a chance to ease back into their relationship, see how things would go? Kanika shook her head. No, that wasn't Tyrell's style. He didn't give you time to rethink your position. Once you were in, you were in for life and he was making no exception with her—especially with her. She reached out and caressed the ring. But could she do it? Could she throw the past, the hurt, the betrayal, and the broken trust out the window?

Kanika took a deep breath and decided. Yes, she could. The truth was, she had begun to forgive Tyrell some time ago. When she kept seeing him come back, again and again and again. When he let her see how unwavering his love for her was. When he let her see how much he not only wanted her, but needed her. When he let her see that he had become a better man for her because of what had happened, she had begun to forgive him. And now she had to decide to trust him with her heart again.

"Kanika?" he said, starting to sound stressed out.

She looked up at him again and then held out her left hand. He stared back at her, almost in disbelief.

"Oh, now you got nothing to say? You going to stand there

looking dumb or are you going to put the damn ring on my finger?"

Tyrell snapped out of it, took the ring out of the casing, put
the box on the night stand. He turned back to her, took her hand
in his, and slid the ring on her finger.

Kanika stared at the ring, feeling happiness spread inside of
her. Then she reached up and pulled him down on top of her.

They made sweet love, and it was the best it had ever been between them. Kanika came so hard that she saw stars. She didn't
even realize she was crying until Tyrell started to kiss her tears
away.

"Promise me we'll always be together, Tyrell," she whispered.

"I promise, baby," he whispered back. "I promise."

She and Tyrell had returned to Brooklyn and their relationship had been better than ever. They had even been blessed with
a six-month-old son Kanika had named Tyrell, after his father,
but they all called him Little T. Kanika smiled and looked down
at her ring. She couldn't be happier.

"Uh, earth to Kanika!"

Kanika snapped out of it to realize that Sheila had been jab-
bering away about something and she hadn't heard a word.

She smiled sheepishly. "Sorry, what were you saying?"

Sheila rolled her eyes and said, "I *said* that Brooklyn is gonna
miss you."

"Well more than I'll miss it! I need some peace. I need a break,"
Kanika said, sitting down with Sheila on the sunny steps outside
the brownstone. "Sometimes I wish Tyrell and I would never have
to come back."

"Don't even go there. What else would y'all do? Work for Veri-
zon? Let's be honest. This is your life, Kanika. It's about time you
accepted it."

Kanika had accepted it. In a few days, she'd be Tyrell's wife, and her life was going to change yet again. She wasn't just a child in the game—she was soon to be married to it.

"Do you know who's moving in?" Sheila asked.

"Some white family bought it. They just had a daughter. They are the only whites living on this block. It didn't even bother them."

"Not for long. The neighborhood is changing," Sheila said. She watched the cars zoom up and down the street.

"Everything's changed. When my mama and Tony died, it was—"

"The beginning of the end—"

"Never," Kanika snapped. "It is the start of a new beginning. You can take all the players out of the game, but you'll never take the game out of the players. This is all Tyrell and I know."

"Me, too, girl. But a lot of people are gone. Just dead or in jail," Sheila said.

Kanika refused to listen. She couldn't entertain those weak-minded thoughts, because they would raise more doubts. In the life she was living, there was never any room for gray areas—it was always do or die.

Kanika's ringing phone disturbed the conversation.

"Hello?" she asked.

But the caller hung up.

Kanika clutched the phone in her hand. "This been happening all day."

"You still have that number?"

"Yup, but I may have to finally change it. I have someone calling and hanging up on me. I have a feeling I know who it is."

Sheila looked at Kanika.

"I know Tyrell will make me change it," Kanika said, looking at her phone again when it rang. "Heelllo?

The person hung up again.

"Whatever," Kanika said.

It rang again.

"Hello!" she screamed into the phone.

"Calm your ass down," Tyrell said with a little laugh on the other end. "What happened?"

"All day somebody is playing on the phone. I think it's Tiffany."

"*Change* the number."

"No, I wanna hear what she has to say. She'll talk eventually."

"I'm getting you a new phone when we get back. Nobody should have that kind of access to you. Case closed," Tyrell said in a firm tone.

Kanika's heart pounded. She loved him even more when he was protective like that. "Where are you?"

"We're on our way," Tyrell said, referring to their six-month-old son, Little T.

Kanika and Sheila went back inside the house to get her luggage.

The rule on Turks and Caicos was that you had to stay on the island for a few days before you could marry. So after three days, they had their ceremony on the beach with Little T nestled in Kanika's arms. Kanika thought it was the most magical experience that had ever happened to her. She finally felt she had gotten the security back that she had lost when her mom and Tony were killed. She had a family of her own.

"You like this?" Kanika asked as she stepped out the bathroom in a sexy pink-and-black garter belt and corset.

Tyrell could only grin.

"We waited a week to have sex, so we might as well do it

right," she said, sitting on his lap. They were on the veranda of their private villa on the beach.

Tyrell caressed Kanika's thighs and kissed her full breasts, which were half-exposed. "I wanna take this real slow tonight."

"I know, this place is so pretty. The water looks like a shimmery black pearl. The stars like icicles. I wish we could live like this every day."

"We can do whatever we want," Tyrell said as he sipped his glass of Henny.

The warm, humid breeze intoxicated Kanika. She felt her whole body tingling with anticipation—they would have the night to themselves in such a beautiful place.

"Uh-oh." Tyrell laughed. "You wanna do it this time?"

Kanika huffed and went back inside to get Little T. He had awakened and needed his feeding. She unzipped her entire corset outfit and gave him her milk. The frustration Kanika felt at going from hot sexiness to a milk machine left her as soon as she saw Little T's happy eyes looking up at her. After she fed him, she burped him and laid him back down. She knew her baby's routine and figured that she and Tyrell would have just about two hours to really do anything.

Maybe a half an hour later, Kanika transformed back into her sexy self. "Little T is a good sleeper, so we got a few hours," she said, handing her husband a glass of champagne. "But these high heels hurt."

"C'mere." Tyrell took her hand and brought her over to him. "You look good enough, I can eat you right here."

"Then go ahead." Kanika unbuttoned the flap to her corset bottom. "Dig in."

"Hold on, though, I wanna sample a lil bit of everything."

"Out here?"

"Yeah, ain't nobody watching us on this patio. Turn around."

Kanika turned around, spread her legs, and bent over. Tyrell massaged the flesh of her ass in his hands. He loved to slap it and make it wave. He bit her gently and she rolled her butt around in his face. She kept her hands on her knees as his mouth got acquainted with her pussy from behind. She put her hand on the banister when her knees started to go weak from the pleasure.

Tyrell picked her up, took her inside, and laid her on the bed. Little T was asleep, so they had to keep their volume low.

He slipped her corset off, slid off her garter belt, and went to work on her body from head to toe. Kanika wasn't in control tonight, but she didn't mind; she lay back and enjoyed the ride. For the next hour and a half, they tended to each other's bodies until Little T woke up again.

*T*oday's our last day," Tyrell said as they packed up a bag to take to the beach.

"That is why we need to get a tan. What's it gonna look like that we've been here seven days and haven't even gotten one tan line?"

"Because we been too busy celebrating—"

"Having sex." Kanika handed Tyrell the baby. "It's gonna be so obvious to folks."

They both laughed and headed out to the private beach. The hotel already had a table of food awaiting them, along with beach chairs and towels.

"Wow, this is crazy," Kanika said, picking one of the grapes. She studied the spread of fresh fruit, chips, chicken salad, finger sandwiches, and a chilled bottle of champagne.

"Well, do you, because I'm about to hit the Jet Skis," Tyrell said, before walking down the beach to rent one.

Kanika was fine with staying behind with the baby to soak in the sun. She wasn't much of a water person and had fun just watching Tyrell zip up and down the coastline. She was glad to see him being so carefree. It was rare for the both of them to relax like this, since they always had to watch their backs.

When the sun got too strong, she and Little T lay under an umbrella while she flipped through fashion magazines. Once in a while, she'd wave to Tyrell. There were a few couples on the beach, all white, mostly older. She felt their glances, but didn't pay them any mind. She wondered if they thought she and Tyrell were some rap or music couple. *That's better than the truth,* she thought.

"Excuse me."

Kanika looked out from under the umbrella. "Yes?"

"Hi, I'm Sam, a villa attendant. I was wondering if you need anything? We are always here to help."

Kanika checked out his villa uniform and looked around. "Uhm, no, we're good."

"I see you are here with your husband?"

Kanika smiled. "Yes, we just got married."

"Is that him on the Jet Ski? He's good."

"I know," Kanika said, looking out into the water. But she couldn't see Tyrell anymore.

"Well, if you need anything, let me know. It's your last day?"

"Yes," Kanika said, squinting her eyes in the glare. "But we're fine. Thank you."

"Congratulations and enjoy the rest of your stay." Sam walked away and looked back only once at Kanika.

She didn't think much of it until Tyrell appeared.

"Who the fuck was that?" he asked, agitated.

"Oh, that was one of the workers asking if we need anything."

Tyrell patted his body down with a towel and shook his head at Kanika. "Didn't we talk about keeping to ourselves?"

Kanika gave Tyrell a confused look. She didn't get it. "He works for the hotel."

"Did you see him talk to anyone else out here?"

"No?"

"Why us, then?"

Kanika thought about what Tyrell was getting at. "Do you think he was checking up on us?"

"Yo, he just came out of nowhere. You never talk to people like that. What was his name?"

"Sam."

"And he just asks you if you need anything? What else he asked you?"

"He asked about you—"

Tyrell threw his towel down. "We outta here," he said, picking up the baby.

Kanika slipped on her shades and got her few belongings. She didn't feel right anymore.

An hour later, Kanika and Tyrell checked out of their hotel.

"Did you enjoy your stay?" said a light-skinned woman with braids in her hair, working behind the hotel checkout counter.

"Perfect." Kanika grinned.

But Tyrell was silent.

"Okay, your car is waiting."

Kanika, Tyrell, and the baby got inside the airport shuttle. But before they got in, Tyrell said to the driver, "I wanna give Sam a special thank-you."

"Sir, there's no Sam who works here," the female driver said. "Is there someone else, maybe?"

Tyrell looked at Kanika, who buried her face in her hands.

Chapter 2

Tiffany sat at her customer service desk at the Citizens Bank on Church Street, filing her nails until the lunch-hour rush. Her mostly unopened office mail was piled high on her desk. She already knew what they were: more loan applications. But she was waiting on something special. It would be in a small white envelope. She waited patiently while the mail boy went around everyone's desk to drop his load.

"Ms. Tiffany, here you go," said the young black guy with tiny dreads in his hair when he stopped at her desk.

Tiffany grabbed the bundle out of his hands. At the bottom was the envelope. She opened it and found the photos she had asked Sam, a man her girl Rasheeda—one of her father's old connects—had put her in touch with to spy on Kanika. Tiffany didn't trust Kanika, since her father had died at the hands of that woman's new husband, Tyrell, one of the major drug kingpins in the North.

She wanted to keep eyes on Kanika, just in case Kanika wanted to finish what she had started. Tiffany thought that maybe Kanika was doing the same. But as she scanned the photos of Kanika, Tyrell, and their baby son on their wedding day, Tiffany realized that she herself was the only one who hadn't moved on. A jealous rage came over her as she saw how lovingly Tyrell looked at Kanika and the way he held her close. One of the photos was solely of a smiling Kanika in a sexy white string bikini, and the baby sitting on a blanket along the beach. Everyone looked happy and refreshed in the photos. Kanika was glowing, and Tyrell and the baby looked peaceful and happy.

It burned Tiffany up to know that Kanika was living such a carefree family life, while Tiffany's own family was dead, mostly because of Kanika. Tiffany studied the photos again. She spotted Kanika's chunky, shiny diamond ring, her designer sunglasses, and Tyrell's studded diamond earrings. They had money, too, she thought. Much more than she did. Tiffany held the photos so tight that they wrinkled at the corners. She was pissed off. She wanted to scream at the top of her lungs that Kanika was living a life that was meant for her, and her alone.

Almost two years ago, Tiffany was riding high because her father was the number one kingpin in the South. Now, since his death, she was on her own, his empire broken up into pieces. Everyone had a piece but her. Kanika and Tyrell had rebuilt theirs. Tiffany thought everything had been stolen from her. But she vowed to get it back.

She dialed Kanika's number again.

"Hello?" Kanika said on the other end.

"Your day is comin', bitch. I hope you enjoyed your little vacation." Tiffany hung up. She had never said anything before when she called, but today was different. She was ready to get things poppin' again and to claim her name.

The little call made her feel a whole lot better as the first lunchtime bank customers swarmed in. As soon as she saw their faces, she lost her energy again. There was no way she could survive another week here.

"What you doing for lunch?" asked Zeesha, one of her co-workers.

"Same ole, probably go to the fried chicken place," Tiffany said as she tucked the photos away.

"Count me in, but I'm so tired of chicken."

"I'm so tired of working here. Tired of these old-ass people who can't read or write. I need to make some real money." Tiffany grabbed another form from an elderly woman waiting to be directed to the proper window.

"I still don't get it," Zeesha said, and chewed her gum loudly. "You are supposed to be sitting up somewhere living off your daddy money. You don't belong here."

"My point exactly, but my daddy didn't have no real bank money. Everything he had, the government took it. They can prove where it came from, so they gonna say that my daddy owed all this back-tax money."

"Whatever. You need to be out there, getting your own."

"I'm finally ready," Tiffany said. "It's been hard adjusting to everything, but hey, I gotta do it. I still ain't have any dick for a minute, too, so I'm all fucked up."

"For real, girl, you need to handle your business."

"I do have some business I need to handle with some folks in New York, and you better believe I will," Tiffany said.

Whose car is *that*?" Tiffany asked Zeesha when they noticed a shiny platinum silver Benz coupe outside the bank on their way back from lunch.

"You don't know who that is? That's Keon. He's always at the bank."

"But I never knew he was riding like that!"

"Girl, Keon is in the bank like every week, dropping mad money," Zeesha said. "I'm a teller—I know all people business."

Tiffany and Zeesha walked inside the bank to their respective work areas. Tiffany peeped Keon's every move. He didn't have to wait on line like everyone else. She had seen him before, but the way he dressed gave no clue to what kind of paper he had. But he was attractive, she thought, with a thick, healthy build in jeans and a red baseball cap and black T-shirt.

Zeesha winked at Tiffany when the bank manager, Steve, who was barely 5'4", came forward and greeted Keon personally. Tiffany thought about how'd it be to get a man like Keon. That was what she needed, too, she thought. She wasn't checking for niggas unless they had cake. No man could compare to the love she had for Saliq, or maybe even his clout, but she had to start somewhere, and not just anywhere—it had to be at the top. She made it her priority to draw Keon's notice before he left.

Tiffany waited until he was done with Steve. She let Zeesha handle the customers who waited, and unfastened the first few buttons of her work blouse.

Tiffany walked up to him. "I'm Tiffany. I'm one of the customer service reps here. Can I help you with *anything*?"

Keon checked Tiffany out in her fitted navy blue uniform pantsuit. His eyes told her that he liked what he saw. "I'm Keon—nice to meet you."

"I was just checking in to see how your experience was today," she said, squeezing her shoulders together so that her voluptuous breasts stuck out.

"It was good as usual. I've seen you around here. Glad you stopped me."

Tiffany licked her lips. "It's no big deal, but I couldn't help notice that you are one of the few men in here who don't need a cane."

Keon laughed. "Really? I couldn't help but notice your beautiful blouse."

"Thank you," Tiffany said, and when she noticed Steve approaching them, she finished, "but don't let me stop you. We'll catch up. Okay?"

"Yeah," Keon said, looking disappointed. He watched Tiffany shimmy her ample rump back to her desk.

After that, she kept her eyes glued to the window to see what car he was going to. He slipped into his silver Benz coupe and jetted off. Tiffany was definitely feeling him now.

"So?" Zeesha asked her from behind the customer service desk.

"He wants to fuck me. I think I'm in love." Tiffany smiled. "He walks like he got a big dick, too."

"He sure does."

"How you know?"

Zeesha rolled her neck. "I'm just playin'."

"That's mine, don't play with me," Tiffany said, giving Zeesha a nudge.

"I couldn't help but notice, too. But there's something different about him."

"What?" Tiffany asked. "He got money. That's all there is to it."

"On his bank record he lists himself as self-employed, and the category is Industries. What the hell is that?"

"That is the code word for the game, girl." Tiffany huffed impatiently. "We can't put down what we really do."

"I don't know. He just don't seem like—"

"Trust me, I know it when I see it. I just need to find out who he's linked up with. He live around here?"

Zeesha plugged some numbers into the computer so they could both scan Keon's file.

"Damn, he's from Maryland. Why he got an account down here?" Tiffany asked.

"He got another account in Florida. He must be really paid to be spreading his money around like that."

"How old is he?"

Zeesha scrolled down the screen. "Forty-two."

"Perfect!" Tiffany grinned.

"You're only twenty-three."

"So, I like them old. That way they can die quicker and I have more time to play," Tiffany said.

Zeesha laughed, and they both analyzed his other data.

Instead of going home to her tiny studio apartment after work, Tiffany headed to Rasheeda's house, a sprawling mansion in one of the best areas in Virginia Beach. Rasheeda had got in touch with Tiffany when she found out what had happened to her daddy. Rasheeda was a thick, curvy chick with almond-shaped eyes, a tiny waist, and full, luscious titties. Tiffany had never been with a woman, but she felt sexually attracted to Rasheeda, as well as to her money and power. Tiffany imagined that her father had hit that, but she wasn't too sure.

Rasheeda turned heads wherever she went. She had a way of talking to any nigga and getting what she wanted. She had a nigga's swagger and wasn't too slow on pulling out on one when she had to. She also owned an escort service, a nightclub, and controlled the drug empire from Virginia to Memphis. She took over after Tiffany's father was killed, but promised Tiffany that if they worked together, Tiffany could come back on top. Rasheeda would help.

Tiffany helped Rasheeda, too, by processing phony loan applications that Rasheeda needed. She must have given Rasheeda thousands of dollars of loans in other people's names. It was Tiffany's access to cash that made their relationship tighter. She admired Rasheeda and wanted to be just like her one day. If she could be anything like Rasheeda, she could be half as good as her daddy, she thought.

"Why do you look like that?" Rasheeda asked Tiffany, who sat across from her in the office den, dressed with burning incense everywhere.

"I am stressed. I saw the photos Sam sent me."

"Me, too," Rasheeda said, frowning. "Ain't it a bitch?"

"I couldn't believe how happy them muthafuckas look while I am here struggling. She's married, got a man who loves her, a new baby, a house maybe, lots of money. This shit ain't fair. I need to come up with a plan."

Rasheeda examined her long orange-and-gold manicured nails and let Tiffany vent.

"I shouldn't have to work at no bank. My father had a name around here. I wanna rebuild what we had. I want people to know my name. And they ain't gonna know my name if I spend all my hours in a fucking cube."

"I thought you wanted to lay low and strike only if they strike?" Raheeda reminded her.

"For a minute, I did. But I don't give a shit about that anymore. I need to live my life, too, and stop waiting for niggas to do something. I need to be on the streets. I miss the excitement. I want the money, the fame, and the glory."

Rasheeda laughed. "Basically, you wanna be like your dad?"

"Better than him if I can. I wanna take back what was taken. You can show me."

Rasheeda leaned in and put her elbows on the desk. "That won't be a problem, but you gotta be ready for this. Once I start schoolin' you, you can't look back. I don't share my skills with nobody."

"I was always ready, but my daddy didn't take the time. He probably thought I was gonna marry some rich hustler and wouldn't have to do shit. I need to know everything it takes to get respect, keep it, and grow fear with it."

Rasheeda raised her eyebrows at Tiffany's determined tone.

"It's time for me to devote one hundred percent of my time to taking back what's mine and for payback. I wanna make sure Kanika and Tyrell wish they never met me. I wanna permanently take that smile off her face she had in all those pictures."

Rasheeda grinned, liking the sound of that. "I was wondering when you'd wake up to your true calling, girl. And I am here to help, like I said. What you need?"

"Anything, at this point. First of all, I need to get rid of this job. I need money. I need a team. I need to know how to shoot to kill, how to make money, all that."

Rasheeda spun her chair around, her back turned to Tiffany. There were a few minutes of silence as Rasheeda thought to herself.

Suddenly spinning back around, Rasheeda said, "Move in."

"With you?"

"Yes, you don't have to go back to work. I can take care of you. Any bills you have, any money you need, I got you. That way we can be close and you can learn by seeing how I handle mine."

Tiffany's body shook with excitement. Her admiration for Rasheeda reached a new level. No one had reached out to really help her since she'd been left alone. "In this house! Oh my God. Thank you so much, Rasheeda. I promise I will pay you back whatever."

"No need to. You looked out for me at the bank. I respected

your daddy. I'm just doing my part," Rasheeda said with a twinkle in her eye.

Tiffany stopped herself from jumping up and kissing Rasheeda. "No one has ever done anything for me—except my daddy, of course, and even he had his moments."

"Girl, enough of all that. I am happy to have you stay as long as you need. What am I doing in this big-ass house all by myself anyway? I don't have a man, don't want a man, and I don't need one. All I need is a little companionship, a friend to talk to, and you can be that," Rasheeda said as she walked Tiffany downstairs to the kitchen.

"Oh, hell yeah!" Tiffany laughed. She wanted to be anything Rasheeda asked.

Rasheeda looked at Tiffany's face. She lightly caressed her chin and jaw. "All I ask is that you don't disappoint me."

Tiffany's body tingled at Rasheeda's touch. "I will never disappoint you, and I'll make sure nobody else ever does either. We will be in this together."

"Good," Rasheeda said. She got out some slices of bread for a sandwich. "Now, taking on Kanika and Tyrell ain't no big deal. All we need is the right access. We need to find out where they are staying."

"I can do all of that. I'm pretty sure they still living in Brooklyn."

"Don't be too sure. After what went down, they probably moved to fuckin' New Mexico. Everybody's been keeping a low profile."

Tiffany nodded. She watched Rasheeda fix a big, meaty turkey sandwich. Rasheeda sliced it and gave Tiffany half. "Speaking of keeping low profiles, there's this dude I see at the bank. He look like he got paper, but no one knows who he rolls with."

"His name?"

"Keon Mason."

"Never heard of him," Rasheeda said, food still in her mouth. "What about him?"

"He's fine as hell. He is pushing a brand-new Benz convertible. Nice lips, too."

Rasheeda sighed loudly. "He sounds like a cornball. If he was anyone, I'd know him."

Tiffany raised her eyebrows at Rasheeda's slight attitude.

"Is he gonna be your new man or something?" Rasheeda asked.

"No, I was just curious. I mean, hell, maybe."

"Look, if you plan to take back your daddy's name and get the respect you deserve, you can't be chasing after no niggas. You think any nigga gave me any of this?" Rasheeda opened her arms wide to indicate her massive home and fortune. "I did it all on my own. I refuse to let any man come into what I have built on my own blood and tears. You should do the same."

Tiffany chewed her sandwich slowly. She took a big swallow and said, "I don't know if I can be without no man. I always had a man around me, from my daddy to my ex, Saliq—who Kanika and Tyrell killed. Now I'm by myself, but not because I wanna be. Shit, I need to feel a nigga dick up on me once in a while—"

"See what I'm sayin'. You need to stop thinkin' about niggas. You are a beautiful bitch, with a fat ass, pretty bedroom eyes, big-ass titties, and a sexy short hair. Niggas will always be sweating you. But never sweat them. Focus on getting money," Rasheeda said, and popped the last of her sandwich in her mouth.

After they ate, Tiffany chilled with Rasheeda for the rest of the evening, watching movies and eating more food. Though Tiffany was only twenty-three, and Rasheeda thirty-eight, she felt a sisterly bond with the older woman. It was a bond she and Kanika, her half sister, never did get right.

"It's almost eleven. I am so damn tired," Tiffany said, yawning.

"Me, too," Rasheeda said, turning off her seventy-two-inch flat screen in the home theater.

"Your place is like a fuckin' resort. I wish I never had to leave here," Tiffany said.

"You don't." Rasheeda walked up the steps to her bedroom while Tiffany stayed downstairs.

"What you mean?" Tiffany shouted. "I gotta get my things from my apartment."

But Rasheeda didn't answer her. After a few minutes, Tiffany followed on up the steps. Rasheeda was standing right there.

"Let me show you around," Rasheeda said, and took Tiffany to the five bedrooms she had on the one floor. "This is the second master suite. This room would be yours."

Tiffany stepped into a room that was three times the size of her apartment. It was painted a deep royal purple, with matching lavender curtains, bedspread, and antique-style wood furniture.

"I love it," Tiffany said. "This must be one of the biggest bedrooms I've ever seen."

"You ain't seen nothing, then." Rasheeda closed the door, and Tiffany followed her to her own bedroom. She flung open the door.

Tiffany gasped at Rasheeda's luxurious sanctuary. It was painted in red with gold trimmings and color accents. The bathroom was big, clean, and sparkling with gold fixtures. But what surprised Tiffany most was Rasheeda's walk-in closet, fitted with every designer name imaginable.

"Wow, this is like a hotel suite or something!" Tiffany grinned and walked over to a cabinet. "What's this?" She opened it.

Rasheeda laughed. "Oh, that's my little collection of videos I made. I like to record myself."

Tiffany picked up one of the videos, which was labeled only with a number. "Interesting," she said as she perused the other regular popular porn titles. There were also feathers, chains, and whips in the cabinet. "It's like a sex shop up in here."

"This ain't nothing. You shoulda seen what I had in my old place, pratically a dungeon filled with shit."

"I feel you, girl." Tiffany laughed, turning to leave but wanting to stay. "Let me go before it gets too late."

"It already is. Why don't you stay? Instead of driving that half hour back home."

Tiffany looked at her watch. She thought she'd rather stay at Rasheeda's place than go back to her cubbyhole.

"Listen, you can use your room, shower, do whatever. It's not like you going to work tomorrow, right?"

"Right, I almost forgot."

"Cool, so go ahead and get yourself ready for bed," Rasheeda said as she led her back to her room.

Tiffany decided to just go with it. She showered in her new bathroom and took pleasure in all the little oils and lotions stocked in there. By the time Tiffany was done, she smelled like lavender. On her bed was a robe and brand-new slippers still unwrapped. Tiffany smoothed her skin with more of the scented lavender oil and slipped on the short black terry robe. She jumped into her bed and pulled the covers to her chin. Then there was a knock at the door.

"Come in," Tiffany said in the dark.

Rasheeda crept into the room. "Was everything okay?" she asked, sitting by the bed.

"Yeah, thank you. I don't know what I was thinking about going home."

"This is your home now." Rasheeda touched Tiffany's smooth hair and gave her a good night kiss on the lips. When Rasheeda left, Tiffany lay there awake for hours, no longer tired.

She thought of her father and how safe and loved he had made her feel by giving her a mere look with his winning smile. Saliq crossed her mind, too, and those nights they'd spent at the Dairy Queen, eating ice cream and cracking jokes on the customers. He'd take her home after, and they fucked for hours. If it wasn't at his place, he'd take her to the cliff, where they'd look out over the stars and the town below. They'd have sex right there in his car, just as if they were the only two people on earth.

He would've done anything for her, and she would've done the same for him. Maybe it was her father's pick of him as his second-in-command that she fell in love with, but she also grew to love him for being his own man. She had the most fun in her life with Saliq, which was what she needed, because her father was always about the business. She and Saliq had their rough times, but he was the only man she'd been with. When she was dead wrong, he had no problem checking her, too.

These were the two men in her life who had made her into the woman she was today, and she wasn't going to let them down any longer. She wanted to be loved again, by anyone.

Chapter 3

I **hate it here,**" Kanika said on the phone with Sheila while she cooked. It had been a week since she and Tyrell returned from Turks and Caicos to their new four-story white-picket-fence home in Upstate New York.

"Didn't you say you wanted to lead a normal life?" Sheila asked.

"Yes, but not in the woods. There are deer around here. I got frogs in my backyard. I mean, it's like *Little House on the Prairie* up here."

"Come on, girl. You were the princess of Brooklyn, you can be the princess of Upstate."

"That don't even sound right."

Sheila laughed. "It don't."

"But how can I tell Tyrell? He surprised me with this when we got back, as my gift. I have a gigantic backyard with a gardener, a wraparound porch, seven bedrooms, five bathrooms, one and a half kitchens, a pool, a Jacuzzi—I have everything. I just don't have Brooklyn."

"You need to be honest. But remember, he did this for *you*. He wants to protect his family and is doing what any man would. Don't be too hard on him."

"I just don't even think I can make friends up here. Everybody on my block is white and old. There are no black people. The moms here all look like they live for the PTA and bake-offs. I ain't like that. I need some excitement."

"Maybe you should try making friends. Has anybody come by?"

"Not yet. But they better not come by with no welcome basket of cookies or I'll throw up."

"Yeah, that would be too *Leave It to Beaver*. But hey, I can always come see you. Tyrell still got the barbershop down here."

"I know, but with the baby and all, I can't be up and around too much."

"I really think you have an opportunity to build a nice life up there. Shit, you may be calling me soon to tell me you joined a book club or something!"

"Hell no," Kanika said. "I like reading what I want to read."

"Never say never."

Kanika noticed that the pot was boiling over with some rice she was cooking. "Girl, let me go and get this dinner ready."

"What y'all having?"

"Roast chicken, wild rice, and cauliflower."

"Cauliflower!"

"I know, another new thing I got to get used to. The produce guy insisted I should try this bland mess."

"Put some hot sauce on it."

Kanika smiled. "All right, girl, we'll talk later."

Kanika continued to prepare dinner for her family. She was already bored with it. They'd had chicken every night this week. When he told her he had a surprise for her, she'd have sworn it was a piece of jewelry or maybe even a new car. Even up to the moment they got out of the car, she was shaking, until he handed her the house keys. She'd cried tears of joy, but it finally sank in that she was out of her element.

"Yo, yo, yo," Tyrell called out when he walked into the kitchen about eight o'clock. He put his arms around Kanika. "I could smell the food from outside."

"It's probably the cauliflowers."

"Cauliflowers?"

"Yeah, some new thing I bought today. I hope you like it." She frowned.

He grabbed her ass in her tight jeans and kissed her on the nose, then lips. "As long as I can eat you later."

Kanika sucked on his bottom lip. "That's for dessert." She grinned.

While Tyrell went to play with Little T, Kanika got the table ready. She placed the plates at their respective spots and prepared Little T's bottle.

"You're feeding him this time while I eat," Kanika said, handing the bottle to Tyrell as they sat around the table.

She watched Tyrell struggle to eat his food and feed Little T at the same time. She loved watching him and their son together. She could feel the love in Tyrell's eyes.

"So, how was your day?" he asked her as he bit into the baked chicken thigh.

"Good but boring," Kanika said, picking at the rice. "How's the food?"

"Excellent. Cauliflowers are the bomb."

"I hate living here," Kanika said without thinking.

Tyrell dropped his fork. "Come again?"

"I mean, there's nothing to do. I don't know anyone. There's no one to talk to when you be out all day." Kanika sliced her chicken breast as she spoke.

"Well, go introduce yourself. Take the baby for a walk or something, I don't know." He shrugged. "On second thought, don't introduce yourself."

"You see what I mean. I have to act isolated around here. At least in Brooklyn, everyone knew what I was about and no one fucked with me. Here, I gotta hide who I really am."

"You really letting it all out tonight, huh?" he asked in a frustrated tone. "I bought us this house so we can have a normal life, so we can raise our son without having to look over our shoulder. You sounding really selfish."

"How? I know what I want."

"It's not about you anymore. It's about us," he said, pointing to the baby. "You need to get used to this."

Kanika ate the rest of her meal in silence. Perhaps he was right, she thought. Maybe, if she made an effort, she could see their new neighborhood in a new light.

bout 10 A.M. the next day, Tyrell drove down to Brooklyn. He had a meeting with his right-hand man, Mike. Only Mike knew where he lived, but Tyrell didn't want anyone to visit him there. He liked to keep his business and his family separate, though the business was also part of his family, of course.

"Shit has been mad quiet out here for a minute," Mike said as they sat in Tyrell's basement office at the barbershop. "I don't like that."

"Me neither. When there's too much silence, there's lots of plotting going on."

"Word. I'm hearing that niggas is still hating on you for what happened with Tony and 'em."

"Yeah, whatever. They'll always think the top spot came too easy for me. That I don't belong here, or Tony is dead because of me. But I'm running shit now. I ain't bowing to nobody. Let whoever have a problem come to me."

"They won't." Mike snickered.

"When they want a job or money on the table for their family, they'll be knocking." Tyrell nodded. "But yo, there's more important matters on hand."

Mike gave Tyrell his full attention.

"I got this little situation in VA. To make a long story short, niggas is looking to get back at me and Kanika for some shit that went down over there. Her half sister, Tiffany, got like a contract out on our asses. I need to shut her down or at least scare the shit outta her so she'll leave us the fuck alone."

Mike shook his head. "So that's what it was—"

"What you mean?"

"Some niggas was telling me that some VA cats were looking for you. They even said one of the cats went to Turks and Caicos."

Tyrell hissed. "Yeah, well, there was somebody there asking about me on the damn island. On my honeymoon. I knew that nigga was shady."

"Word, them VA niggas got they eyes on you already. We need to shut them down now."

"Not now," Tyrell said, leaning back in his chair. "Too much drama, too soon. It's gonna make me lose money. When there's blood, there's no green."

"True, true," Mike said.

"So, I wanna pace this out. We can send a signal to their inner circle. But as long as my family is safe, that's all that matters," Tyrell said.

"I know just who to hit, too. It'll have them thrown off guard for weeks."

Tyrell pulled out a wad of cash from the drawer. "Here, go pay everybody tonight."

Mike got up, then turned around. "How's Kanika?"

"She good."

"Peeps is asking about her, too. They saying how she just dumped everybody to go live the high life."

Tyrell laughed. "Tell them she's living in the motherfuckin' White House now."

When Mike left, Tyrell sat in his office and turned off the lights. Sometimes he liked to sit in the darkness. His heart still had a heavy, dark weight to it. It bothered him that Kanika wasn't happy. Since the day he told her about how her mother died he promised that he'd never make her cry anymore. Any pain she felt, he felt more. It was a burden he was ready to carry for life. He could never leave Kanika, he thought, even if she wanted him to.

He turned on a small lamp and pulled out a blood-speckled handkerchief. It had Tony's blood on it. It was what Tony had had in his pocket the night he was murdered. Tyrell had played the scene many times in his head and wondered what would've happened if he had been there, if he had played it cool and not been so insistent with Tony about things. Tony was about nonviolence, and his passive tactics were outdated in the volatile drug game. They were about to be destroyed by a rival Colombian gang if it wasn't for Tyrell. Tyrell reasoned that if he hadn't stepped in and taken Tony down, they'd all be dead. And he was right.

Tyrell kissed the cloth. He said a silent prayer, hoping Tony would bless him and Kanika and have their back, because sooner or later, things were going to get heated.

A*re there* any collard greens?" Kanika asked the produce man at her local supermarket.

"Sorry, they won't be here until next week," said the round sandy-haired man. "Nobody buys them anyway."

"Next week? What is this, a third-world country?" Kanika huffed as she pushed her cart down the aisle. She eyed the asparagus and picked up a bunch.

She rolled her eyes as she pushed her way down the aisle with Little T in the cart. Lots of shoppers glanced in her direction with fake smiles. In her small neighborhood, she stood out, even at the grocery store. There was one main supermarket in town. Kanika was impressed with the selections, but missed some of the products she was used to. As she roamed the aisles, she tried to connect with some of the other black shoppers, but everyone kept rolling along.

She stopped by the meat counter and surveyed all the different cuts. This wasn't what she was used to. She had never talked to a butcher before, and always got her meat straight from the frozen-food sections. She listened in as others placed their orders for lamb, duck, pork, rabbit, pheasant, beef, and chicken.

"No, no, no," she heard a little elderly black woman say as she pointed to the butcher man. She looked elegant in white silk gloves, a fitted black trench coat, and matching hat with a white trim. "Don't cut my beef where you just cut the pork!"

"Sorry, ma'am," the young guy said. He looked new to this.

The old lady sighed in annoyance, watching him like an owl. "Good." She smiled when he gave her the neatly wrapped packets of meat. "Thank you."

Kanika looked away from the old woman because she didn't want to seem like she was staring.

"Young lady, just make sure he doesn't cut your meat on the pork side. White people don't care, but I do," she said, pointing to her chest.

Kanika laughed, amused by the feisty old woman. "Okay, but I have to think of what to order. I'm tired of chicken, and I just don't know how to order."

"It's a matter of trust. You can ask them what they think is best for whatever meal you want. Or you need to come prepared with the cut and portion size you need."

"Well, I want lamb chops tonight."

"Then ask for the lamb chops, prime or choice."

"Okay." Kanika smiled curiously. "I'm Kanika. You are?"

"Oh, how rude of me," the old woman said. "I'm Delores. Nice to meet you. Do you live around here?" Delores leaned down and played with Little T's small hands. "He is adorable."

"Thank you. We live on St. Marks Street."

"I live there."

"I live at 5567."

"5559," Delores laughed. "On the same block."

Kanika laughed, too. "Another black person?"

"Indeed! Are you here alone?"

"I live with my husband and son," Kanika said as she and Delores talked it up while other shoppers walked past them.

"Where did you guys come from?"

Kanika felt her insides freeze. She remembered Tyrell's warning about talking too much. "We came from nearby," she said, and began to push her cart slowly. "But it was nice meeting you."

"Oh yes, and you should stop by sometime," Delores said before Kanika disappeared around the corner.

Kanika went back to the meat counter and ordered the lamb chops just the way her neighbor had instructed.

Chapter 4

"Oh, shit!" *Rasheeda yelled* a week later when she hung up the phone. "Tiffany!"

Tiffany ran down the stairs when she heard Rasheeda scream her name. "What the hell?" she asked.

Rasheeda paced the floor in her office, clearly agitated. She beat her desk several times. "They got my second in command, Teeko."

"Who did?"

"I'm not even sure. We had some beef with niggas from Memphis, but that's not they style. Whoever did this decapitated Teeko. His baby mama didn't even recognize his body."

They stared at each other.

"I don't know anybody who get down like that, but it's possible it could be somebody you don't know," Tiffany said, and her mind tossed around the idea that Tyrell or Kanika was behind it.

"You think Tyrell did it?"

Tiffany didn't think that was too far-fetched. "Why not? He and Kanika hate me. They'll do anything to see me down. I wouldn't put it past them."

"But you haven't even been fully anointed yet. Nobody knows you are about to take over your daddy shit. Why they after my shit?"

"Because they know we connected."

Rasheeda breathed down hard. "Well, that nigga don't want none of this. I got your back one hundred percent against that fool. But something is telling me it ain't him."

Tiffany knew that she'd have more clout and power to get back at Tyrell if she could get Rasheeda on her side. "It's him. I'm telling you. That nigga is a fuckin' nut. He killed his wife's own mother."

Rasheeda grinned. "Shit, I should have him on my team."

"Never," Tiffany said, folding her arms across her chest.

"I understand why you hate Tyrell, but isn't Kanika blood?"

"She used to be, until she played me. I ain't got no problem going after blood."

"You know, Kanika went to school down here for a minute. She is well respected. That girl is fly as shit. I've seen her a few times. She's gorgeous."

"What that got to do with anything?"

"I'm saying that you gotta pick your battles. She got a strong network. If you fuck with her, not only will Tyrell come after you, but so will all her little fuckin' cronies. *You* wanna be the one they respect, not her."

"So how do I change that?"

"You gotta be smart about it. That's why I said let's see what happens before we do anything. You gotta make a name for yourself again. You gotta remind them that Kanika had everything to do with your father's death and that you are back to stake your claim. You gotta let them know they're the bad ones and you're not."

Tiffany nodded her head. "I'm feeling that. If I can get some-one on their team to be on my team, that'll be big."

"Hell yeah, and I know just the person. We'll talk about it."

Tiffany sat down. "What you gonna do about Teeko?"

"Me, or you mean us?"

"Us."

"I'm gonna fall back for a minute. We ain't ready to strike yet. Not until I can show you a thing or two. You gotta earn your posi-tion, girl. It's like starting from scratch. New niggas done took over your daddy shit, and it's been broken up into little pieces. Once you take care of that, we can do our thing together. But I gotta see that you have heart. Standing up to that nigga Tyrell is gonna take more heart than your daddy had."

Tiffany felt shaken, but she was ready to do whatever. It could be the difference between simply killing Tyrell and Kanika and taking over their empire, she thought.

"Are you ready? Because what just went down means war."

"I am. I wanna make sure they'll never forget my name. I wanna destroy Kanika and make the bitch bleed. And I know just how to do it."

"How?"

"Take what she loves."

"Well, if you gonna be the head bitch, it's time you start look-ing like it, too." Rasheeda pulled out a long black case and gave it to Tiffany.

When she opened the case, she saw a thick lioness platinum pendant encrusted with yellow diamonds. It came with a match-ing eighteen-inch chain. "This is hot!"

"My uncle Joe made it for me when he was working for your daddy. He passed it down to me. I had a matching one made just for you." Rasheeda helped Tiffany put the chain around her neck.

"Nice." Tiffany laughed as she checked herself out in the mirror. "This is exactly how I'm supposed to be rockin'."

Then Rasheeda slipped the chain off her neck. "Like I said, you have to earn your place, starting tonight."

A *round midnight*, Tiffany and Rasheeda went to the local Waffle House for a late-night meal. It was a popular hangout spot for heads to go to before the club. They shared jokes and laughed as they stuffed their faces. It reminded her of what she missed. She was starting to like Rasheeda, and it was important that Rasheeda liked her, too.

While she ate, Tiffany saw Keon walk in and place an order by the counter.

"Keon," Tiffany called, waving over to him. "That's the dude I was telling you about from the bank," she told Rasheeda excitedly. Rasheeda didn't seem impressed when he walked up to them.

"What's up?" He grinned and extended his hand to Tiffany and Rasheeda, but Rasheeda didn't shake his.

"Hey, what are you doing here?" Tiffany asked, eyeing his iced-out Rolex watch.

"Same thing you doing here."

"At least I got some company. You don't have a woman at home with you tonight," Tiffany said, licking the chicken grease from her fingers.

Keon's eyes followed every motion of her lips. "Uhm, nah, I'm chillin' by myself tonight." He looked at Rasheeda uncomfortably. "Why?"

"Maybe I can keep you company," Tiffany said.

Keon blushed as he looked at Rasheeda again, who seemed like she was choking on a bone. She coughed profusely.

"You okay?" Tiffany asked, reaching over and patting her back.

Rasheeda nodded and turned to Keon. "Tiffany's busy tonight."

Tiffany gave Rasheeda an icy glare. "Oh, yeah, I forgot," she said to Keon, feeling bad.

Keon looked confused. He took out a paper and pen and gave her his number. "Well, whenever you get a chance," he said, and walked away.

"That chicken was crazy," Rasheeda said as she pushed her plate away.

"Why'd you do that?" Tiffany asked.

"Girl, please. You *are* busy tonight."

Tiffany looked at Rasheeda sideways. "What you talkin' 'bout?"

Rasheeda paid the waitress for their meal, said her good-byes to those in the spot who recognized her, and took Tiffany for a ride.

"This is what your daddy used to own. All up and down this neighborhood."

Tiffany peered out the window at the makeshift houses and sheds while Rasheeda drove. "These people are dirt-ass poor, some of these houses ain't even got windows."

"They used to, but they all crack houses now. Your daddy used to run this whole section back in his day. This was big money down here."

They rolled up to a grassy area where there was a single shed with one window. The lights were on. A few crackhead prostitutes wandered by and banged on the window for cash.

Tiffany hadn't seen this part of town in a while. She didn't miss it. It was a place her daddy hardly ever frequented unless he had some ass to kick.

"Here," Rasheeda said, and handed Tiffany a cold 9.

"What is this for?"

"Tony Nino is in that shed right there, right now with two of his boys. See." Rasheeda pointed them out to Tiffany.

"Yeah, I see 'em. They look like they playing cards."

"They smoking crack. And Nino is the one who took over most of your daddy's spots. The others will be over, once they hear what happened."

Tiffany listened.

"You gonna go in there and blast Nino. Pop your clip on that fool."

Tiffany stroked the cold metal with her hand. She felt a rush of adrenaline, but she didn't know how to use the gun. "I'll do it. But how?"

Rasheeda took the gun from her. "All you have to do is aim, put your finger on the trigger, and shoot."

"Like this?" Tiffany took the gun and aimed it toward the dashboard.

"Nah, you trembling. Look, put your hand high on the gun, like this." Rasheeda showed her. They got out of the car. "Stand somewhat sideways with one foot in front of you, lean your shoulders forward, and bust off."

Tiffany took the gun back and practiced by pointing the gun away from them.

"Good," Rasheeda said, standing behind her with her hand over Tiffany's on the gun. "Make sure you got a strong stance—it'll help you aim better."

After a few more minutes, Tiffany got the hang of it. "What now?" she asked Rasheeda when they got back in the car.

"You do this tonight, then everything is yours. Word will get around, and you'll have niggas wanting to work for you." Rasheeda opened up Tiffany's car door and nudged her out.

Tiffany stepped out into the cool April evening. The grass

tickled her calves as she slowly walked step by step to the shed. Once there, she bent down to get a good look at everyone. But she realized something. She didn't know who Nino was. She panicked and wanted to run back and ask Rasheeda. But the car was too far, and she didn't want Rasheeda to think she was looking for a way out.

She cocked her gun and watched the crack pipes stuck to the lips of the men inside. She didn't know Nino. Rasheeda must've forgotten to tell her which one he was, she thought. Whoever he was, Tiffany was disgusted that her daddy's empire was now being run by crackheads.

Tiffany's hands began to shake. She thought that the trembling would fuck up her aim. She focused on her hands and waited until they relaxed. She barely remembered anything Rasheeda had said on how to shoot. On a count of three, she blasted all three men. They tumbled to the ground. She caught one of them in the head, and she didn't stop until she ran out of bullets.

When she was done, two bodies lay on the blood-drenched floor, and another light-skinned taller man was bent over the table with his eyes open. Blood spatter painted the walls and soaked the cards they'd played with. One of the men's hands was clutched around a crack pipe. She walked up close to the window to see it all, but didn't want to go inside the place for fear she'd get herself gory with the carnage. Tiffany breathed quickly though her mouth. Her neck felt stiff from how tightly she held her shoulders together. A single tear streamed down her face. Only one, she told herself. She wasn't going to let anyone see her at a weak moment. She wiped the tear away, ran back to the car, and sped off with Rasheeda.

This was a high like she had never experienced before. She patted her chest, tried to catch her breath. "Why didn't you tell me who Nino was?"

Rasheeda looked over at her. "Because if I did, you'd only kill him, and that's not how you make a name for yourself. You make a name for yourself by doing the unexpected."

The following night, Tiffany and Rasheeda celebrated big-time at Paradise. Rasheeda had officially dubbed it Tiffany's "coming out" party. Since what went down the night before, Tiffany felt untouchable. There was a newfound invincibility that even made her walk differently. Her back was straighter, and her gait was more self-assured. She looked people in the eye, almost daring anyone to test her. She did what many people, including men, couldn't do. That was a cause for celebration in her eyes. Rasheeda had the club shut down just for her peoples, and everything was on the house, including endless bottles of Moët and Cristal.

Tiffany was nestled at a table in the corner with Rasheeda, Deyqwan, her right hand, and Jermaine, another one of her runners. All four drank from flowing champagne glasses and ate chilled jumbo shrimp as they laughed, joked, and listened to music. Tiffany excused herself to the bathroom, but stopped in her tracks when she spotted a familiar face.

"You again," she said, patting Keon on his back. "What you doin' here?"

Keon's face brightened up. "What's up."

She felt better than him, better than most of the people in the club. Her life was too busy, she thought. While others played the sideline, she was getting hers in.

Keon just stared.

Tiffany said, "You didn't answer my question."

"Oh, my boy said this was the place to be tonight, so I said why not. Good to see you." Keon savored Tiffany's skintight black bodysuit.

"Who's your boy?"

"Derrick. Right over there."

Tiffany noticed that Derrick was actually a friend of a friend, and no one special himself. She had hoped that Keon had some connection to the game, but he didn't. He seemed like a regular dude, and she was interested. He was earning money the right way, she thought. Something she didn't mind trying. Just when she was about to say something, Tiffany heard Rasheeda call her name.

"Listen, I'll be back. Don't go anywhere," she told Keon, and walked back to their table. She turned around and caught Keon watching her move with his bedroom eyes.

"Girl, we gotta introduce you tonight. Come with me on the stage," Rasheeda said, grabbing Tiffany's hand. "Then when this is over, there's business to attend to.

"Everyone, shut the fuck up for a minute!" Rasheeda laughed, spilling her champagne on the floor. Jermaine ran up and poured some more in her glass. "Shut up!" she shouted for a final time. The DJ cut the music, and everyone dropped what they were doing.

"This is my girl, right here. Tiffany. I guess y'all heard what happened up in Boxter the other night, right?"

Several voices yelled out in support. Tiffany saw everyone's approval, and she liked that. She tried to find Keon, but couldn't.

"Anyways, she is the one taking over the family business. Her daddy was a fucking king around here, so now y'all can meet the queen," Rasheeda said, pushing Tiffany out in front.

Tiffany didn't say anything, but smiled back as everyone clapped and cheered. After a minute, she walked off the stage with Rasheeda.

"What the hell was I supposed to say?" Tiffany asked her.

"Nothing, just be you. Besides, the people we really need to talk to are already waiting to talk to you after this."

"They are?"

"Yeah, I got you a whole team of people. You need niggas like I have, someone to do the dirty work in the street. You know the deal."

"I do, I do." Tiffany grinned. A popular Snoop Dogg song came on that threw the club into a ruckus. Tiffany and Rasheeda waved their hands with everyone else as they moved to the beat. When it was over, Tiffany made her way to the bathroom again. She looked around for Keon and finally spotted him at the exit.

"You leavin'?" she asked him at the door.

He eyed her with a mean grille. "I told my boy I was out when I found out what this really is about. You down with this?"

Tiffany cocked her head to the side. "Excuse me? I know you ain't tryin' to judge. Don't act like this is brand new to you."

"What's that supposed to mean?" he asked, straight-faced.

"It means you must be doing something to get all that money you have. You know exactly what this is about. And yes, I am down with this. It's my life."

Keon shook his head like he'd heard enough. "I make my money the old-fashioned way. As a matter of fact, I sell real estate. I've been doing it for ten years. That's where my money comes from. And yours?"

For the first time tonight, Tiffany had come down off her high. She was hurt that here was another man trying to run away from her, and not get to know who she really was under the hard face. The life that brought her so much validation also took away almost anyone she'd ever cared for. Keon was a chance to be with someone different, and there she was again. But she had to be strong, she told herself. "Look, you can go. Whatever. You proba-bly couldn't handle all this ass anyway," she said, swishing her hips as she walked to the bathroom.

When she returned to the table, Rasheeda asked, "What's wrong with you?"

"Nothing, just niggas pissing me off as usual."

"I saw you talking to that cat at the door. What he saying?"

"That's Keon, the nigga I asked you about. He actin' like he too good for this party. Telling me he makes his money the old-fashioned way." Tiffany filled her glass with more champagne. She wanted to be as drunk as possible before the end of the night.

Rasheeda whispered something to Deyqwan, who quickly left the table.

"Where's he going?" Tiffany asked.

"To check out your boy."

"Girl, please, Keon is a square. He can't hurt nobody." Tiffany laughed nervously. She knew what was about to go down, and she could stop it, but she didn't. "Bet next time he'll think twice before he talks."

A few hours later, Tiffany and Rasheeda walked downstairs to the basement, where there was a meeting. Rasheeda introduced Tiffany to some of the men who would be on her team.

"Rock and Darnell will be the ones working with niggas in the street. They'll do whatever. You just say the word," Rasheeda said.

Rock and Darnell were both six feet tall and well built. She wasn't so attracted to either of them, as she'd hoped. They nodded in her direction and left the room.

"And finally, the next one is gonna be your right hand. He'll be dealing with me a lot, too. But basically he keeps you happy. Communicates with Rock and Darnell on what they need to do. Yo, Lexus!" Rasheeda shouted.

The next thing Tiffany saw was a six-foot-two man dressed in an all-white outfit with a white fedora. His skin was dark and powerful. "I'm your angel in disguise," he laughed as he and Rasheeda hugged. Tiffany tingled inside.

"How you doin'?" she said, impressed by him. She was magnetized, and by the way his eyes stayed glued to her face, she could tell he felt the same way, too. After a few more words were exchanged, he left, as well. Tiffany and Rasheeda were alone.

"Now, I saw how you and Lexus were checking each other out. Don't do it," Rasheeda warned her.

"Why? I mean, ain't he supposed to be at my beck and call?" Tiffany teased.

"Because once you start fuckin' these niggas, they wanna take over. They get all high on themselves. Trust me. I've been there," she said as they walked back upstairs. The club was emptying out, and everyone was chilling in the parking lot. "And I fucked him."

Tiffany stared at Rasheeda with a cold face. "Is that why?"

"No, it ain't. I just want you all to myself." Rasheeda laughed.

Tiffany walked behind her, confused, but decided that maybe it was best she kept it strictly business with Lexus. When they got in the car, Tiffany asked Rasheeda, "Where's Deyqwan? He never came back."

"Oh, he had to take care of Keon. They kicked his ass outside the club and dumped him off somewhere."

"Is he dead?"

"Hell no. Just fucked up. We couldn't leave his body out here all bruised. You know how five-oh be looking for anything."

"True," Tiffany said, a chill shooting down her spine. She wondered if she just made her first order.

Chapter 5

Kanika bundled up Little T and hustled down the block to visit Ms. Smith. She wasn't even sure how the old woman was going to react to her surprise visit, but she couldn't take another minute in the house alone. She was bored out of her mind.

"It's Kanika from up the street," she said when she heard Ms. Smith at the door.

The door flung open with Ms. Smith smiling on the other side. "What took you so long? Come on in."

Kanika was relieved that Ms. Smith was so happy to see her. As soon as she stepped in Ms. Smith's home, she felt the love and warmth emanating from the yellow, red, and wood tones all over. There were large oil paintings of a couple hanging on the walls, and the woman looked like Ms. Smith, but in her younger years.

"Have a seat, darlin'. Are you hungry?" Ms. Smith asked as she walked into the living room with a pitcher of lemonade.

"No, thank you, ma'am. I just wanted to stop by—"

"Don't call me ma'am." Ms. Smith winked. "I'm Delores."

"Okay, Delores. Your house is so lovely."

"Not as lovely as this precious little boy," she said, gently brushing Little T's cheeks. Little T offered up a smile. "How are you?" Delores asked. "You know you been on my mind since I met you a few weeks ago."

"Well, it was really good to see another black person. I'm just not used to living in surroundings so quiet. Nothing is going on here," Kanika said, and rested Little T in the crook of her arm. He was dozing off.

"Where are you from again?"

"Brooklyn," Kanika said, forgetting Tyrell's rule.

Delores's eyes squinted as her perfectly painted tiny mouth pouted. "That can be a bad area."

"Bad as in good. I miss my neighborhood. I need some action." Kanika laughed. "I miss the sirens!"

Delores laughed, too. "Well, I grew up in Harlem. I know what city life is like. What does your husband think?"

"He loves it here. He wants it to be quiet."

"What does he do again?"

Kanika hesitated. "He works for himself. He has a barbershop."

"Well, I don't mean to be rude, but tell me how can barbershop money afford the houses around here? We're talking high six figures or more, right?"

"Much more. But he's very smart."

Delores smiled faintly. "You see these oil paintings? They're of me and my late husband, Errol. Errol was one of the biggest hustlers in Harlem in my day. He ran with the best, until he took over the rest. He became the number one man for many years. Until the feds came and destroyed our lives. Errol was never violent, and we used the money and we did some wonderful things for the community. He then bought us this house right here. He died in jail ten years ago."

Kanika rocked Little T in her arms. She couldn't look Delores in the eye. "Why are you telling me this?" she asked.

"Because I know the life when I see it. You two are very young. Probably the youngest couple on this block. Right?"

Kanika nodded.

"And you have so much."

"Couldn't we have gotten it the right way?"

"Did you?"

"No," Kanika admitted. "So, I guess you know what my husband does now. I understand if you don't want to have anything to do with us—," Kanika said, leaving.

"Dear, no," Delores said, and stood up. "Sit down."

Reluctantly, Kanika did.

"I was just trying to explain to you that I know what you're going through. It's a hard life. It's like the higher they climb, the more isolated life becomes. I live here all alone, no family, no friends. It was just me and Errol. No kids."

Kanika felt depressed. But she thought maybe this was something she needed to hear. She missed having an older person's perspective. Now she missed her mother even more. "I know what you mean, Delores, but these are different times—"

"The game never changes—people do. I just try to warn young people to stay focused. And for you, sweetie, just try to get used to living up here. I'm sure your husband has his good reasons."

"He does." Kanika nodded. "I've always had so much growing up, and he just wants to keep giving it to me. I just sometimes feel—"

"Trapped?"

"Sometimes, but I can't think of any other life—"

"Me neither." Delores smiled as she poured Kanika a glass of lemonade.

By five o'clock, Kanika had already prepared the night's dinner of veal, green beans, and rice. The table was set, and she sat Little T up in his chair. As promised, Tyrell turned the lock on the door right on time.

"Where my people at?" he asked as he walked through the house.

"In the kitchen!" Kanika shouted.

Tyrell walked in, scooped Little T up, and planted a fat kiss on Kanika's lips. "Mmm, something smells too good to eat."

"It is good, and you're gonna like it." Kanika fixed their plates as they sat around the table.

"You in a good mood." He smiled.

"For now," Kanika said. She fed the baby a bottle and fed herself at the same time. She and Tyrell normally took turns doing this.

Tyrell tasted the veal and frowned. "This ain't chicken."

"No, it's veal. I wanted to try something different. Just anything to add some life around here."

"*Veal*," Tyrell rasped. "But I'll eat it because I love you."

"I love you, too. So you better lick the plate."

"But why?" he asked as he chewed the food.

"I told you."

"You could've made spaghetti."

Kanika rolled her eyes and flipped Little T over to burp. She tasted the veal and wondered why she had never made it sooner. It was delicious. She could tell by the way Tyrell was chomping on it that he liked it, too.

"So what you did today?" Kanika's words dragged out.

Kanika took a sip of juice from her glass. "I made a friend today."

"No wonder why you cheesin' like that. Good. So, who is this
person? Like a PTA member or something."

"No."

"Okay—" Tyrell raised his eyebrows.

"She's an older black woman I met at the supermarket. She
lives right up the block, and I went by with Little T."

Tyrell chewed and nodded. "Black?"

"Yup. I was so happy to see someone I have something in
common with. And guess what. Her husband was a big-time hustler in Harlem. His name was Errol something. He ran the drug
game up there for a while in her days."

Tyrell stopped chewing.

Kanika held her breath for a moment. "Don't worry—I didn't
tell her what we do, but she may put two and two together."

"Why the hell she telling you that? You opened your big mouth
again?" Food flew out of his mouth. "It's the same shit you did in
Turks and Caicos, opening your damn mouth. You couldn't meet
a regular person, but you had to meet someone who we got something in common with. We don't want to be close to anyone. You
can never be too careful, the way we live."

Kanika clenched her jaw. She understood what he was saying.
For all she knew, Delores could've made everything up. What if
she could hold the information against her, she thought. But
then a small part of her was angry, too. "If I had someone to talk
to, if you were even around more than half the time, maybe I
wouldn't be out there talking to strangers!"

Tyrell stood up. "Who the hell you think you yellin' at?"

Kanika put Little T down in the playpen next to the table.
"Who else is standing here?" she asked him.

"You know what, I can't take this shit. I give you a life many chicks would die for. We live in one of the best homes anyone could want. You ain't got to work. You got Louis this, Gucci that—you got it all. A man who fucks you, feeds you, and takes care of you. And that ain't enough?"

"I hate it here!" Kanika exploded.

"You just a spoiled-ass brat." He pointed in her face. "I think you better fall back right now."

Kanika glanced away from his stern look. He turned her cheek to face him.

"And if I ever hear you telling anyone what we do, I'm gonna beat your ass," he said in a cool, calm manner.

Kanika pulled her face away again. She wasn't afraid of Tyrell, but she didn't want to disrespect him further. She remembered seeing times her mother and Tony would hand fight, and make up days later. It was how they handled their disagreements, and it may be how she and Tyrell had to get down sometimes, she thought. But it wasn't like she was waiting for it. All she wanted was peace. "Look," she said, calming down. "I want us to get at least an apartment closer to the city. We can keep this place, but I need someplace else to go to."

Tyrell took her into his arms. "I didn't know it was messin' with you like this. I'll see what I can do. I can't make any promises."

Kanika, Tyrell, and Little T spent the following afternoon shopping at the local mall. Retail therapy was exactly what she needed. Tyrell took her on a spree at Nordstrom, where she spent thousands of dollars on new jeans, a newly arrived Louis Vuitton bag, three pairs of Jimmy Choos, and three stylish Chloé blouses and matching shades. He also bought Little T at least half a dozen cashmere baby outfits. It was the end of winter, but there were a few more weeks for Little T to rock his new wares.

Kanika and Tyrell stopped for ice cream in the lower lobby of the mall. They grabbed a pair of seats in the corner of the open-air cafeteria. A couple of black girls walked by in skintight jeans shorts, baring their bellies with short halter tops. Kanika peeped Tyrell looking as the girls walked past the table. He strained himself not to turn around.

"Go ahead," Kanika said, licking her spoon. "Do it. I know you want to."

"What? Them chicks? Please, I got all I need right in front of me."

Kanika swirled her caramel ice cream in the cup. She had thought about this many times, but never asked. "Do you think about being with other women?"

Tyrell scratched his light goatee. "You want the honest answer?"

Kanika nodded.

"I do. But it's different than how I used to think about it. I'm married—I ain't dead."

"What do you think about?"

Tyrell smirked. "I think about you. Then maybe how it'd be with someone else. It's just fantasy. I think about Stacey Dash if I see her picture. Stuff like that. I ain't checkin' for nobody, if that's what you mean."

Kanika forced a smile. She didn't want to scold him. "I did mean that. I guess it's okay to fantasize. I do it, too."

Tyrell leaned across the table. "Who the hell you be fantasizing about?"

Kanika smiled. She could tell he was jealous. She loved it, but she couldn't think of anyone he would believe. "Just guys. I'm married—I ain't dead."

Tyrell caught on and popped a grin. "I wanna be the only man you think about."

"Will I ever be the *only* woman?"

"You are *my* woman. I wanna be the one you fantasize about. So what's your fantasy?"

Kanika looked around at the crowded tables. She didn't have a fantasy she wanted to share right then and there. But it wasn't like they spoke on these things every day, she thought. "I wanna have sex in public."

"That's it?" he asked.

"You?"

"I wouldn't mind seeing you with another girl."

Kanika stuck the spoon in her mouth. *Hell no,* she thought. She wanted to slap the taste out of his mouth. "Are you serious?"

"Are you?" he asked.

Kanika wasn't all that comfortable with the idea, but she wanted Tyrell to feel comfortable talking about these things. They were married, and she knew her mother would remind her of her duties as a wife. "If you really wanted to, I would."

"I wouldn't want to force you."

"No, you wouldn't." Kanika smiled. "I'd probably need a drink before it all goes down, but I'd do it. I'm curious. But I would have to be in total control."

Tyrell's face lit up.

"I would have to pick her out myself and it would have to be out of town, like vacation or something."

"You ain't gonna pick some obese fat bitch, are you?" He smiled.

"No," Kanika said, slightly covering her face. "I'd want her to look like me. Bad. Beautiful. Nice ass."

"Why we gotta be out of town?"

"Because what happens out of town, stays out of town," she said, and dumped her empty ice cream carton in the garbage with his. "You ready?"

"Yes, ma'am," Tyrell said as he took her hand and pushed the stroller. "So, how you feel about living here now?" Tyrell asked as they walked out to the parking lot. He had a sarcastic smile plastered on his lips.

"A little better. Honestly, I didn't even think they had these kind of stores. But I still want us to be closer to the city," she said, and playfully batted her lashes. She noticed that Tyrell's faced turned serious. "What's wrong?"

"Nothing, but—" While they stood at the garage elevator door, he held the baby. "I just feel weird. I felt weird all day."

"I'm sorry about yesterday. Maybe this place will grow on me or something," Kanika said.

"Nah, I mean, it's me. I feel like something is about to happen."

Kanika stared at him intently. "What do we do?"

Tyrell exhaled before entering the elevator. "Let's just get home."

Kanika followed Tyrell to the car when they got to their parking level. Tyrell was a very intuitive man, and whenever he didn't feel right about something, he was on point. But Kanika couldn't pin down what it could be. She hoped everything was okay back at the house.

As Tyrell sat the baby in the carseat, Kanika felt a chill go up her arms, and then three masked men ran up on Tyrell, put him in a choke hold, and stabbed him several times.

Kanika screamed, but realized she didn't have her gun on her. She checked the glove compartment for Tyrell's, but he'd gotten to it first. Shots rang out then, and the men scattered and ran.

"Get in the car!" Kanika yelled. She grabbed Tyrell's gun from him and helped him limp toward the car before pushing him in. She hit the gas and sped out of the lot.

Kanika shouted as she checked Tyrell out in the mirror. "We need to go to the hospital now!"

"Hell no," Tyrell mumbled. He began wrapping his arm with an extra baby blanket he'd gotten out of a backseat pocket. "Too many questions. Same reason why we can't even call the cops."

"Tyrell!"

"We can't," he said with his eyes half-closed. "I still have a bullet in me from the last time I was jumped. I can fix this."

Kanika's eyes were red. As she drove, she saw Tyrell do exactly what he said. He was stabbed in his arms mostly and in the side. He had wrapped himself up completely, and when they got home, she tended to his wounds with a mixture of witch hazel, honey, and lemon juice, a concoction her mother had used on Tony for years.

Chapter 6

*I*t *was* *Friday* *night.* There was a major party being given by some NBA players, and that meant Rasheeda's escort service was in demand as usual. Tonight, all the top girls were at Rasheeda's house for the pep talk.

"Okay, bitches, y'all got a busy night ahead. Rayna, you meeting Deon Minton at the hotel at three A.M. He wants it all. Everything. This time, bring the extra dildo for his ass. Got that?"

"He usually uses mine, why I need to bring a extra one?" asked Rayna, a caramel-skinned sister with blue eyes and a black curly weave.

"Because the nigga asked! He's paying six thousand dollars tonight. He could ask for a motherfuckin' blow doll, for all I care. He's getting it. Don't fuck up."

Rayna nodded. "I got something for his ass, all right."

Rasheeda cleared her throat. "Now, the rest of you got your appointments down. Don't be late. You be at the hotel before they get there. Already ready, already washed, pussy salivating. Understand?"

Everyone in the room nodded in unison. Tiffany could tell, watching from afar, that Rasheeda really had the girls on a tight leash. They looked like they wouldn't dare cross her, even if they could.

"Michael Miles is gonna be at this party, and he wants you to meet him there. Stay in the car," Rasheeda said, handing a card to Ava, a slender Hispanic girl.

"I'm done," Rasheeda said as she raised her hand in the air. She checked her pager. "Y'all better get to it. All tips in cash, please!"

The ladies walked out of the house in a straight line of lace stockings, bodysuits, halter tops, booty shorts, and heels. There was something for every man's taste, from the reserved to the scandalous.

But another escort, Diana, a slim light-skinned girl with a short cropped afro cut stayed behind. Tiffany peeped that.

"Are they gonna have all the fun tonight?" Diana asked Rasheeda, who whispered in her ear.

Tiffany walked down the steps when she heard them laughing out loud.

"We have our own plans tonight. Besides, you know I always pay you full price with benefits." Rasheeda playfully slapped Diana on her jiggly ass.

"What y'all talking about?" Tiffany asked.

Rasheeda grunted. "Nothing you'd understand."

Diana rolled her eyes.

"How come you didn't go?" Tiffany asked Diana. She wasn't feeling her. Tiffany had hoped she would be able to chill with Rasheeda tonight.

"Boss lady needs some attention tonight." Diana winked at Rasheeda.

Tiffany shook her head. "Whatever." She didn't quite pick up on what was happening.

Rasheeda opened her mouth to say something, but the cell phone rang. "Yes?" she said into it.

"What happened?" Tiffany got curious after a while.

Rasheeda laughed uncontrollably and hung up the phone. "Girl, somebody just stabbed Tyrell up."

"Tyrell?"

"Yes! Niggas stabbed his ass. Too bad he got away, though."

Tiffany was disappointed. "He not dead?"

"No, but looks like someone wants him dead. Someone besides *you*," Rasheeda said, smiling.

"Well, you know what that means. He got beef."

"Yup, and it ain't just with us," Rasheeda said, fixing herself a glass of Hennessy. "You know, I think we should find out who did this. Get them on our side. Use that person against him. We need people who know him. That's the only way we can get close."

"That is so true," Tiffany said as she brushed past Diana, who sat there lighting a cigarette. "We have to use his enemies against him."

"That nigga probably got so many haters right now. Even if we did catch his ass, anybody could be guilty of it. He'd never know it was us."

"So we gotta plan this out right now. While he's hot!" Tiffany said, sitting down on the couch.

Rasheeda put her arms around Diana. "Not tonight. It is late, and I am tired. Right, Diana?"

Diana nodded and followed Rasheeda up the stairs.

"But we gotta talk business!" Tiffany shouted.

"We just did. I got you, girl. Just leave it to me," Rasheeda said. She disappeared with Diana to her bedroom.

A few hours later, around 4 A.M. Tiffany got restless. Lexus came to her mind. She imagined him on top of her and working her body down to the bone. She reached for her phone and was about to dial him, but then she heard the strangest sounds. She leaped out of her bed and put her ear to the door. The sounds were coming from Rasheeda's room.

Tiffany tiptoed down the hall. It sounded to her like Rasheeda and Diana were laughing. Smoke from incense escaped from the spaces around her bedroom door. The door was cracked slightly, and Tiffany peeked into the dimly lit room. Diana's mouth was stuck between Rasheeda's thighs.

"Ooh, whee." Rasheeda laughed gently as she cupped Diana's head. "Go ahead, girl. You are *baaad*," she said to Diana with her legs in the air.

Tiffany wanted to walk away, but she couldn't. Her earlier guess was on point, she thought. Diana was more than just another of Rasheeda's escorts. She fixed her gaze on their naked bodies as they rolled around the bed feeding on each other. A strange sensation came over Tiffany. She was angry and jealous because she thought Rasheeda had liked *her* in that way. Though Tiffany had never been with a woman, she wanted to be Diana.

*T*iffany didn't know what to expect in the morning. She felt like her best friend had disowned her. She was embarrassed for having these feelings for another woman, but she hadn't grow up with a mother or any female she could look up to. She wasn't sure if she wanted Rasheeda or wanted to be her. Either way, what she was feeling wasn't normal. She left the house before Rasheeda and Diana woke up. She drove to Rasheeda's office. She wanted to be someplace where she could clear her mind and think of her new game plan.

"What are you doing here?" she asked Lexus, who was in the

upstairs part of the club, smoking a blunt. He put it out when he saw her.

"It's six A.M. Early bird gets the worm," he said.

Tiffany flicked the lights on. "Where's the worm?"

"It's coming," he said with a smile.

Tiffany thought that working in the office could wait until later. Lexus looked good in his loose-fitting jeans, a white tee, and a white cap. She drank in his presence. She wanted him to make her feel sexy and needed again. She wondered how close she should get to him.

"You got a girl?"

"I got *girls*." He laughed, taking in Tiffany's breasts, which showcased her nipples through her thin white tank. "I see you got some, too."

Tiffany stuck her chest out. "What if I told you I got a thing for you?"

"Do you?"

"Maybe. I realized it last night. I was laying in bed and you came to mind. That was after I heard Rasheeda fuckin' a bitch."

Lexus laughed. "You didn't know she rolled like that?"

"I had my ideas, but I wasn't sure. I really don't care, but she shouldn't be the only one in the house getting some."

"Man, Rasheeda will always be Rasheeda. Is that why you here so early?"

"Somewhat. But I really need to get my game plan in place. I may need you to do some dirt for me," she said, inching closer to him.

"That's cool. You just say the place and time."

"Some business in New York, but I'll get back to you about that. But for now," Tiffany said, biting the edge of his ear. "Do you want this?" Somehow, she felt that was the only way she could keep a man's attention. She put her hands in his lap.

Lexus's shoulders tensed up. "I thought you were talking about business."

She ignored his comment. "I need someone to lay next to me at night and make me feel not so alone."

Lexus stood up. "I can't see a chick like you feeling alone. I didn't think there was that side to you."

"I still got feelings—it's just nobody ever really asks about them," Tiffany said, afraid to look him in the eye. "I need a strong man in my life like I used to have."

"I can do that if you let me." He reached for her.

Tiffany stepped back. "Not yet. Right now, I set the rules."

"Fine with me, but everybody needs somebody sometimes." He grinned. "I'm feeling you like you feeling me. I felt you from day one. Word."

"Let's handle business first," Tiffany said. "Nothing comes before that."

O*n Tiffany's* way back home, she stopped at Lucy's Diner for a box of fried chicken and bumped into Zeesha from her old job.

"Hey, girl!" Zeesha called out from one of the booths. She got up and walked toward Tiffany at the counter.

"How you doing?" Tiffany said. She really just wanted to go home. In her world, there was no more room for little people like Zeesha.

"Good, good. Look at you all decked out. Leaving the job sure been good to you," Zeesha said as she gazed at Tiffany's gold chain and bracelets. "It's only been a few months."

"I don't waste no time gettin' mine."

"Where you stayin'?"

"I'm staying in the area. How's work?"

"Working at that bank is so wack. It ain't the same since you left. I ain't got nobody to scheme with. I need to be like you, girl!"

Tiffany paid the cashier. "You just live your life. Everybody ain't meant to be running the streets like me."

Zeesha smiled. "Have you seen Keon?"

Tiffany tried to play it off. "Who?"

"Keon. The nigga with the Benz coupe from the bank."

"Oh, that nigga," Tiffany said, and hit her head as though remembering. "I think I saw him at some spot."

"That is weird because he came into the bank the other day looking bad, like he had been beat up. He withdrew all his money and closed his account."

"Wow, that's messed up," Tiffany said, glad to hear that at least Keon was alive.

"Well, looks like he's moving. That's another one that bites the dust."

"Oh, believe me, he is better off leaving than stayin'," Tiffany said, and walked out.

Zeesha followed her. "Tiffany, where you work at now? Did you go back to doing what your daddy did?"

Tiffany looked up at the sky. She wanted Zeesha to disappear. "I did. It was the only way I can live how I want under my own terms."

Zeesha stepped closer. "You think I can work for you?"

Tiffany laughed. "Girl, no. This is something you need to be born with. It gotta be in your blood. I can see you getting all nervous and shit. Fuck no!"

Zeesha looked hurt. "It's been really hard for me at work. My mom is hitting me up to pay her back. My credit card bills are crazy. I need your help."

"Help?"

"Can you lend me some money, at least?"

Tiffany opened the car door, took out her wallet, and broke Zeesha off with $1,500. "Can this help?"

"Yes, thanks," Zeesha said, staring in surprise. "I can pay you back."

"No way," Tiffany said, and slammed her car door. "Just take it as all those times you covered my ass when I was processing those loans."

"Girl, it must feel good to be you. You paid!"

Tiffany laughed as she left Zeesha in the dust.

*R*asheeda was home when Tiffany returned about an hour later.

"I was looking for you. Where'd you disappear to?" Rasheeda asked as soon as Tiffany walked through the door.

"Taking care of business," Tiffany said as she marched her way to the kitchen.

Rasheeda followed her.

"What did you do all day? Just gettin' out of bed?"

"Girl, no. I been up since like noon. I couldn't sleep."

"I bet you couldn't," Tiffany said, chugging down some orange juice.

"And that means?"

"Nothing." Tiffany didn't want to call Rasheeda out. She didn't feel it was her place, or at least not yet. "How did last night go with the girls?"

"Fine. I didn't get any complaints. My girls are the best girls in the business. I need to open a School of Hoe-ly Arts. Those bitches keep me paid nicely with their skills. In a couple of weeks, there's a big birthday party for Keshon Miller, that NFL player. All his boys will be down here."

"Wow, he's the highest-paid player in the game right now. Can I meet him?"

Rasheeda grabbed the orange juice from Tiffany and poured herself a glass. "He's married."

"So?"

"He's gay."

Tiffany cut her eyes at Rasheeda. "I don't get you."

"You don't have to! Who else is gonna show you that we gotta keep our worlds very separate? What's it gonna look like, you dating some NFL player? People gonna go into your background when you date celeb types. You just need to chill and focus."

Tiffany sat down on one of the bar stools around the kitchen island. "I just didn't really expect all of this happening so fast. I killed three men, and I didn't even blink."

"Exactly, girl. You are doing the damn thing. What we need to do is get you up in New York. I already have some folks looking into that."

"I never knew my daddy controlled so much of this. Can I ever be like him?"

"Yes, when you get Tyrell and Kanika. You gotta destroy them."

"But what about me? After I do that, what do I have left?"

"Me."

Chapter 7

Sometimes I wish Tiffany could be normal," Kanika said as she and Tyrell lay in bed. It had been several weeks since his stabbing, and she hadn't had a decent night's sleep in all that time.

"She can't be," Tyrell said.

"We didn't even mean to kill anyone that night. Things just got outta hand. Why do I have to be the one with the crazy half sister?"

"I don't think Tiffany's crazy. Crazy people are victims of their own creation. Tiffany is just born evil. The moment she met you, she hated you."

"That's a fact," Kanika said, thinking back. "I just wish we could put this behind us. Can't she see what her father tried to do to us? She couldn't see that evil man she was living with?"

"It was her father."

"I understand, but he was no good to her either. Shit, he even tried to bust a move on me, his own flesh and blood."

"What kind of move?"

Kanika wondered if she should've brought it up. "Forget it."

"Tell me," Tyrell said, embracing her.

"He tried to come at me one day. Let's just say he forgot that I was his daughter."

Tyrell tightened his hold on Kanika when he felt the pain in her words. "I never regretted what we did to that muthafucka. We just gotta finish what we started."

"We didn't start any of this!"

"Yo, relax. It ain't nobody gonna come up in here and do anything to us. Me getting stabbed was a fluke. It could be anybody."

"Tiffany wants to kill us. She doesn't have to do it with her own bare hands, but she has people."

"She don't have the kind of people we got."

"I just wanna handle that bitch one on one, woman to woman. I should go down to VA myself—"

Tyrell turned to look at her. "Are you crazy?"

"Maybe. I don't play with anyone who fucks with my family."

"I got a plan. Just let me handle all this."

"It's not just about you. It's all of us. You and I work together. I told you I ain't gonna be some hustler's wife and keep my mouth shut. I run things as much as you do."

"Not everything."

"You should consult with me. You did come into *my* family's business."

"Yeah, and you'll never let me forget it."

"Well, then, I wanna be treated like an equal. I wanna know what you have planned."

"No," Tyrell said, and turned his back to her. "Did Tony tell your mama everything?"

Kanika thought about it. "Maybe not, but—"

"*But* nothing. It's my job is to protect my family. It really don't make sense to have two people fuckin' paranoid all the time. You need to take care of our son. Something may happen to me one day—"

"Don't say that," Kanika said, walking her fingers along his back. "And you be feeling paranoid a lot?"

"Of course," Tyrell said, turning over. "You are all I think about."

Kanika kissed his mouth, sucking on his thick lower lip. She worked her way down to his dick and sucked him until he moaned. "You taste so good," Kanika said as she massaged Tyrell's dick in her hands. She wiped her mouth and climbed his tall muscular body. He caressed Kanika's smooth, silky body, rolled her over, and kissed her from head to toe. By the time he was done, Kanika's body was limp. He slipped inside her with ease as their bodies rocked back and forth at 6 A.M. Little T was still asleep. It didn't matter what time they had sex, Kanika and Tyrell just could never get enough of each other.

Tyrell collapsed beside Kanika, and they caught their breath.

"You do a good one-armed fuck." Kanika laughed. His right arm was still healing from the stab wounds.

"It's only been three weeks, and it looks much better."

Kanika wrapped her legs around him and snuggled her body into him. They rested for a few minutes, until the phone rang.

"Are you gonna answer it?" Kanika asked.

Tyrell hissed. "Hello? This better be important."

Kanika tried to listen in on the conversation, but it didn't last long. "Who was it?"

Tyrell gripped the cell phone in his hand with a blank stare.

"Tyrell?" Kanika shook him. "Who was that?"

Tyrell jumped out of the bed, slipped on his jeans and a shirt. "It was my boy Sincere. They know what happened. Mike did it."

"Mike was behind the stabbing?" Kanika's mouth hung open. "So what are you gonna do?"

"Just stay here. I can handle this."

"Tyrell, please," Kanika begged as she followed him naked to the door. "Don't go. Just let—"

Tyrell practically pushed her off him. "Get in bed."

"Tyrell!"

But the door slammed shut. She hated not knowing. They lived a life where anything could happen at any moment.

Tyrell didn't want Kanika to worry, but he knew if he told her what he was about to do, she *would* worry. Mike had been his boy for years. They had even come up on Tony's team together. He was one of the last few whom Tyrell thought had his back. He drove to Brooklyn, enraged. Sincere had said they already gave Mike an ass-whipping and were waiting for the rest of the orders from Tyrell. Besides orders, he had something else for Mike.

W*here he* at?" Tyrell practically busted down the door to his office. Mike was tied to a chair and gagged. Sincere and Lolo stood guard. Tyrell flipped out his machete and held the edge of it to Mike's shivering, bloody face.

"Why, man?" Tyrell asked as he slipped on some latex gloves.

Mike struggled to talk. Blood streamed from his mouth. Several of his teeth were knocked out. When he opened his mouth, Tyrell grabbed his face. "I'm gonna show how it feels to have a knife go through you to the bone."

Tyrell scraped Mike's face with the machete, taking off big chunks of skin. He peeled away the skin from Mike's forehead, nose, and lips. When he was done, Sincere poured a case of red ants all over Mike's face. He let out a cry that sent chills through the room.

"Take him to the pier," Tyrell ordered, dumping his gloves in the trash. "You know what to do."

Sincere and Lolo scrambled to get Mike's mutilated but still living body up the steps and in the back of the car that waited outside.

They drove all the way down to the Brooklyn Bridge. There was a pier that the Mafia and other crime bosses used to get rid of "weight." Sincere opened the trunk, but as they got ready to get Mike out, they heard sirens.

"Yo, forget this nigga," Sincere said to Lolo as he popped open the trunk. "Five-oh is on our ass."

"Shit!" Lolo said. Mike's legs were moving. He was conscious. The police lights shone in their direction as they ran off.

W*hile Tyrell* was gone, Kanika took Little T over Ms. Smith's house for lunch. Ms. Smith told her that she'd fix her something special.

"I hope you like chicken salad," Ms. Smith said, and scooped some onto several bread slices.

"Oh, I do, with just a little paprika." Tiffany salivated when Ms. Smith sliced the sandwiches into neat little squares.

"Well, I'm glad you do, because that's all I got!" Ms. Smith laughed. "I had some chicken and a few other things and thought some little sandwiches would be nice to do. I also made a bowl of spring salad with a little oil and vinegar."

Kanika followed Ms. Smith into the living with Little T. Ms. Smith carried a tray of sandwiches, while Kanika held the salad bowl.

"Don't worry. I also have dessert. I made my homemade carrot cake," Ms. Smith said. They put the food down on the table.

"Love carrot cake!" Kanika said. She rocked Little T in her arms. "I could taste it right now. Cream cheese frosting?"

"Cinnamon cream cheese frosting. I made that, too." Ms. Smith laughed.

Kanika thought that it brought Ms. Smith some added joy to be able to make others happy. So far, Kanika thought Ms. Smith's life was pretty lonely, and she was glad she could bring a smile to her face more than once. Ms. Smith brought her something, too, a chance to escape.

As they sat around the dining room table, eating sandwiches and salad, Kanika and Ms. Smith got better acquainted.

"How did you learn to cook like this?" Kanika asked. She forked up some of the light, moist carrot cake and bounced Little T on her lap.

"Honey, I spent so much time in the house, I had to learn something. So I bought some cookbooks and got busy." Ms. Smith reached for her glass of homemade lemonade.

"I don't think I've met a woman who likes cooking. I know I'd rather go out to eat more often if I could."

"I remember my husband and me walking along the little cafés along the streets in Madrid. I think it was there I fell in love with food. Cooking came later."

"You went to Spain?"

"Of course, even though my husband was a drug king, we took time to enjoy our lives. Besides, it was a lot less hassle for him overseas. It was our place to live the true high life."

Kanika stared down at Little T, who seemed to be fascinated by the shimmery gold button on her yellow blouse.

Ms. Smith tilted her head to the side. "Have you and your husband traveled?"

"We got married in Turks and Caicos. But that was short. I do wish we had time to really enjoy life, but we're always on the run."

"Anytime you need a sitter, I am here. Your son is just a angel. I don't think I've met a child yet who can go without crying for an hour straight."

Kanika kissed Little T on top of his head. "He's my angel. The only thing that keeps me calm these days."

Ms. Smith put down her glass. "Just take it easy, dear. I was a lot older than you when I got involved in the street life. I was a college graduate and came from a good solid family with a strong father in the house. I still wandered. At your age, I was still typing away at the district attorney's office. No one thought I'd end up with who I did."

Kanika smiled. "District attorney?"

"Yup, I was a secretary. I helped them get the bad guys and I ended up with one. But I knew the man behind the mask. My husband was a gentle soul. He was just a hustler who needed a way to survive in a time when black men had nothing."

"You think times are different now?"

"Yes," Ms. Smith said in definite manner. "People these days want to get rich quick. They don't know how high the price is. Do you know?"

"I think I do," Kanika sighed. She wiped some cream cheese frosting from her fingers with a napkin. "I'm paying it now."

Ms. Smith folded her hands on the table. "Like I said, I am here if you need me. You can trust me."

When Kanika returned home, she found Tyrell on the couch, staring at the ceiling.

"So what did you do?" Kanika asked with a hand on her hip.

"I did what any real nigga would do."

"Where's Mike now?"

"Let me put it this way: He won't be bothering us again."

Kanika sat beside him and touched his face. "You look bad. I can see it in your eyes. You are tired, Tyrell. We can go far away from all this—"

"We can't," Tyrell said, squeezing her hand. "It is what it is. I just can't get over the fact that it was that nigga. Here I am, thinking that Tiffany and her people did this."

"Yeah, she had me for a second. But don't sleep."

"I know, I'm just feeling sick right now, yo. Mike and I grew up together."

"I understand that," Kanika said in a soothing voice. "But better him than you."

"Word. I just never had to do nothing like this. I mean—"

"You didn't have to kill someone you trusted. I know. But Mike had to go. Thank God we found out about him or he'd still be smiling in our face."

"We gotta move," Tyrell blurted out.

"Because of what happened?"

"We can't be at a place where people can find us. We need more than one home. Mike knew where we lived."

"I was saying that all along."

"But for the wrong reasons," he corrected her. "I can get us an apartment in the city. We can move back and forth. We'll still keep this house. But right now, I gotta watch our backs extra tight. I don't know who else got our address."

Kanika smiled. "I'm with that."

Chapter 8

About a month later, Tiffany and Rasheeda chilled by the pool on a Sunday afternoon. They sipped rum and Cokes while Rasheeda's maid, Annette, bought them whatever they wanted to eat. It was like being away at a tropical island. Tiffany couldn't get over how much money Rasheeda had, and she herself wasn't too far behind now. Rasheeda taught her how to pull in an easy six figures on a weekly basis, taking over small spots and turning them into her own. She had a team that was as hungry as she was and was stopping at nothing to get that cake.

Rasheeda slid off Tiffany's shades as she moved her chair next to hers. "Sleep?"

"No, just thinking," Tiffany said, admiring Rasheeda's black-and-white bikini top and bottom. Rasheeda's body was perfectly sculpted, like she spent every day in the gym, but she didn't. Tiffany thought she didn't look bad either in her purple-and-blue one-piece, which was cut out in the back. It made her short, thick legs look long.

"Don't stress. You doing good. The only thing you need to remember is to never ride alone and avoid confusion on your team.

Confusion causes chaos. Orders have to be clear, and they got to know who is in charge."

Tiffany bobbed her head in agreement. "I just want to make this work. I'm basically learning by doing."

"There's no handbook for this." Rasheeda laughed and slapped Tiffany's thighs. "From what I hear, you doing good in the streets, girl. Keep pulling in that paper. The more you take over, the higher your price goes, the more money we all make."

"So that's it, huh?" Tiffany said, twirling her long gold chain around her finger. "That's probably how Tyrell got so much of his paper, because he's the only nigga left up there. You heard anything about him and what happened?"

"Not yet." Rasheeda lit a cigarette and looked up at the cloudy sky. "But we will. Let's get inside."

Tiffany and Rasheeda grabbed their towels and shoes and rushed in from the impending rain.

"Who's that?" Rasheeda asked when she heard the bell ring.

"I'll open it," Tiffany said, and walked to the door. Annette had already left for the day. "Who are you?" Tiffany asked a man on the other side of the door.

Rasheeda pushed her away. "Can we help you?" she asked with enough attitude. The man's face was badly bruised and deformed. When he only stared, Rasheeda slammed the door. But it rang again immediately. She grabbed her gun and threw it open. "Now what?"

"Tyrell," Mike murmured. His speech was impaired slightly. "I wanna work with you."

Rasheeda looked at Tiffany, who had a big grin on her face. "Well, come on in," Rasheeda said.

Mike walked in slowly with a disheveled black T-shirt and baggy low-slung jeans.

"Sit down," Tiffany said, helping him. Her smile quickly disappeared. "How can you work with us looking like that? You can barely walk."

With the gun still in her hands, Rasheeda sat down, too.

Mike struggled to smile. "How you think I got down here? On a boat?"

"How did you?" Rasheeda asked, securing the towel wrapped around her.

"Long story, but Tyrell and 'em think I'm dead. Niggas found out and tried to kill me, but I escaped. Now I wanna finish that nigga off. But I can't do it alone."

"What you need?" Tiffany asked.

"I was hoping you can tell me what y'all need."

"We want that nigga head on a platter!" Rasheeda said, waving her gun in the air.

"Wait, wait." Tiffany held her hand up. "I'm thinking we can do this differently. I mean, Tyrell ain't the easiest guy to get. And I want to hurt Kanika more than she could imagine. I want to take something away from her that is so precious."

"Her baby?" Mike asked.

"Exactly," Tiffany said.

Rasheeda listened carefully.

"I wanna kidnap that little son of a bitch. You can help me do that, right?" she asked Mike.

"No question," Mike said, and slumped down in the sofa. "But they don't live in Brooklyn no more. They Upstate."

"Upstate? Where Upstate?"

"They got this crib up there, sort of like this. Real nice house. Fireplace, Jacuzzi—"

"Okay, okay, spare me the details," Tiffany huffed. "What I gotta do?"

"I'll take you up to New York, and we'll scout the area. Making sure we can do what we can do."

"Hell, nah." Rasheeda laughed. "Y'all tryin' to kidnap a baby? Then what you gonna do with the baby once you get him?"

Tiffany didn't know. Neither did Mike.

"That plan is not going to work. And I don't think that baby need to be with any one of you. If you gonna go that route, you might as well hold the baby for ransom."

"Ransom, right, right," Tiffany said. "I can bring Kanika and Tyrell to their knees, and they'll give me whatever I want."

"When you wanna do this?" Mike asked eagerly.

"Does he know you alive?" Tiffany asked.

"Not a clue," Mike said.

Tiffany nodded. "I'm ready whenever you are."

Two days later, Tiffany and Mike were cruising up and down Kanika's block.

"How can you not know the fuckin' house!" Tiffany shouted at Mike.

"I ain't never been to his house before. Nobody has. I just know it by the streets I heard him say."

"So how we know we on the right damn block?"

"Because I know the in-between streets. Trust me on this. We'll find it," Mike said as he made a U-turn.

"I don't care if I have to knock on every door on this block," Tiffany said. "I'm gonna find it for real!"

Mike drove slowly as Tiffany looked out the window. "Stop the car," she said, and jumped out. She started with the first house on the block, where an old white woman looked at her like she was a ghost. The next one was the same. Nobody even seemed to know who Kanika was. Tiffany kept trying and knocking. When she reached the sixth house, she was about to give up until she saw an elderly black woman stand outside her door. Tiffany ran across the street.

"Hi, ma'am. Can you help me?" Tiffany asked, walking up Delores's front steps.

Delores quickly turned around as if to go inside, but Tiffany called out to her again.

"Do you know Kanika? She lives on this block."

Delores looked at Tiffany up and down. Already, Tiffany wasn't feeling Delores's cold look.

"Who are you?" Delores asked as she eyed Mike in the waiting car.

Tiffany rolled her eyes. "I am family. I know you know where she lives."

"I don't," Delores snapped, and slammed her door.

"Bitch!" Tiffany shouted, and threw a large rock at Delores's door. "I'll beat your old ass if you come back out here!"

At that moment, Tiffany saw the mailman. She rushed across the street. "Uhm, hi, I'm looking for a Kanika. You know where she lives?"

"Yeah, right over there," he said, pointing to a house halfway down the block. "The red-and-white house."

Tiffany signaled to Mike to follow her in the car as she walked down to the house. She walked around the back of the house and noticed that the grass looked like it had been growing for weeks without attention. She checked the mailbox, but it was empty. She peered through the windows, and all the blinds were closed.

"What's up?" Mike said as he walked up the steps to the porch.

"She ain't here."

"Word, this place looks dead."

"At least I know where she lives. It's mad quiet around here. We can do what we need to do late at night and make it happen," Tiffany said. They walked back to the car.

"What if she was home?" Mike asked.

"We wasn't coming to see her today, but just scope out the area. It looks like it would be mad easy. Bitch don't even have bars on her window."

"And I know how to get through any security system," Mike boasted.

They drove off.

*T*iffany didn't know what she was walking into when she returned home the next morning. As soon as she stepped in, she heard Rasheeda yelling behind Diana.

"I wanna know where all the goddamn money went, bitch!" Rasheeda said as she spun Diana around.

Tiffany walked in slowly and stood by with a grin. It felt so good to see Diana get screamed on.

"I gave you everything I had," Diana cried, backing up a few steps until she hit the wall.

"Is you doing special favors for that nigga?"

"No, I swear, he told me what he told you—"

"So, why was you there until this morning? The call was only for three hours. You were supposed to be outta there by midnight. He had a game today!"

"Look, I did go when I was supposed to. We was in the room together for the three hours. Afterwards, he wanted me to stay and—"

"You stayed?"

Diana hesitated. "I didn't want to—"

Rasheeda cold-slapped Diana across her mouth. "What you think I'm running, some kind of free-fuckin' service? You better go get me my money, ho!"

Diana held her face and looked at Rasheeda with a deep hate. "We didn't do anything. I just laid there next to him."

"Is you insane? I'm supposed to believe that shit? Okay, we'll see," Rasheeda said, dialing Deon Minton's phone number.

Diana face lost any color it had.

"Deon? This is Rasheeda. One of my girls, Diana, said that she stayed extra with you, slept next to you, and did nothing. True?"

Tiffany wished she was on the other end of the phone. She wanted to hear every word Deon had to say and watch Diana crumble.

"Thank you!" Rasheeda said, and hung up her phone. "Nigga said you sucked his dick and fucked him in the ass all night!"

"What!" Diana was at a loss for words.

But Tiffany could tell Rasheeda was lying through her teeth.

"You owe me exactly seven thousand five hundred dollars for those extra ten hours you was with him," Rasheeda said, folding her arms across her chest.

Diana grabbed Rasheeda's arms as she pleaded. "Please, Rasheeda. I swear, I didn't do nothing but sleep next to that man. He's gay. He don't want me."

"He told me what happened. I want my money."

"I didn't leave, because I was tired and it was late. He offered me to stay—"

Rasheeda yanked her arms out of Diana's hold. "Diana, either you get me my money or else."

"Or else what?"

Rasheeda grinned. "Or else, I'll put your ass back on the ho stroll where I found you."

Diana looked faint. Tiffany thought she was about to collapse.

"I'll get the money. I'm so sorry, Rasheeda, but I swear—"

"Tonight!" Rasheeda said, dismissing Diana with a flick of her finger.

Tiffany stood by and watched Diana leave like a sad puppy.

"Whew!" Tiffany said, walking into the kitchen where Rasheeda was. "Glad that wasn't me!"

Rasheeda laughed. "Girl, please. Diana and I have been fighting like this for years. I love that girl. She knows it."

Tiffany shot a surprised look at Rasheeda. "She sure looked like it was the first time."

"Diana is scared of me, and that's how I like to keep it. She knows what she gotta do."

"How she gonna get you the cash?"

"She'll get it doing what she does best: stealing."

Tiffany shook her head.

"I'm going to bed," Rasheeda said, and grabbed a mug of juice.

"It's only noon."

"I just need some time to be alone."

At 9 P.M., Tiffany knocked on Rasheeda's door. She knew Rasheeda was still in a bad mood and was hoping she could make it better.

"Need company?" Tiffany asked. She was dressed in her black nightie.

"I need a massage," Rasheeda said. She rolled over on her stomach.

Tiffany mounted Rasheeda and poured some almond oil on her smooth skin and rubbed her tense shoulders to relaxation. She worked her way down to the curve in Rasheeda's ass to the inside of her thighs. Before long, she and Rasheeda were tied up together like a pretzel, taking turns pleasing the other.

S*everal hours* later, at 3 A.M., Tiffany got news through Mike where Kanika and Tyrell had moved: Manhattan. As soon as she got word, she called a meeting with Lexus over at the house. He came within minutes.

"We gotta be really neat and quick about this shit," Tiffany explained as she and Lexus sat in her new office while Rasheeda slept.

"You just say the word," Lexus said, rubbing his hands.

"Have you ever kidnapped anyone?" Tiffany asked from behind her desk. She'd changed into fitted jean skirt and white tank and sneakers.

"Well, if you count my baby mama. Yeah, I kidnapped her. Then she got pregnant." He laughed.

"I'm fuckin' serious. Now, did you?"

"No, I haven't. But that shit should be easy. All I gotta do is cap Mommy and Daddy. Take the baby."

"That's not how it's going down," Tiffany said angrily. "I don't want to touch Tyrell or Kanika. I want them to be very alive and healthy to feel the pain of having their only son gone. You gotta catch the baby alone."

"So, a little six-month-old is gonna be chillin' somewhere solo?"

"Watch your damn mouth because you fuckin' with my nerves. He got a sitter, some nanny-type lady. Now, I don't care what happens to that bitch, as long as we get the baby from her."

"I wasn't that wrong—somebody gotta die."

"I'll take care of Kanika and Tyrell myself. But I need to know, can you handle this?"

"What kind of question is that?"

"Because you are known for your shooting skills. This is not about that. This is gonna take brains and speed. Understand?"

Lexus nodded with sincerity. "I got you covered."

"Good." Tiffany exhaled. "I just need to get more details, but this is gonna go down with both of us. I'm gonna be there at every step."

"What about Mike?"

"Mike is chillin' up here. Nigga is all fucked up. He can barely walk. He also has to stay out of sight because if Tyrell and 'em ever know he's behind this, it's all over—and I'm just getting started."

Chapter 9

On **Wednesday afternoon, Tyrell** drove out to Brooklyn from their new apartment in Manhattan. He and Kanika were renting out a duplex in a building known for its extended stays for business executives. They had both thought it was a lot less paperwork to deal with, and they wouldn't have to wait to move in. They needed to move given the Mike incident, but at the same time, leave enough room to go back Upstate when they were ready.

But as he arrived at the barbershop, his usually strong instinct was nagging him again. He felt wrong about something. He nodded to the fellas in the shop and headed straight to the basement office. As soon as he settled in, his phone rang.

"What up?" he said when he heard Sincere's voice.

"Yo, uhm, we need to talk to you for a minute. Me and Lolo."

"I'm here, come on in." Tyrell held his breath.

Sincere and Lolo walked in like they were about to be court-martialed. "We need to talk, man," Sincere said.

"So talk," Tyrell said.

Sincere stepped forward. "Uhm, we found out that, ahh, Mike is alive."

"Da hell?" Tyrell twisted his face in confusion. "You niggas didn't dump his body like I ordered!"

"We tried, but five-oh was coming up on us," Sincere said. He turned to Lolo for support, but Lolo looked away.

"You dumb-ass niggas probably went to the other side of the pier. The pier I had sent you to ain't got no five-oh anywhere. They ain't nobody ever there unless they one of us. How da hell y'all fucked up like that?"

Sincere and Lolo stood silent.

Tyrell grabbed the heat from his drawer. He cocked his gun underneath the desk. "So basically, you put my family's life at risk because you heard some fuckin' sirens?"

"I'm sorry, man. I just got off parole and—"

Tyrell blasted Sincere in the head. Brain matter flew everywhere. He pointed the gun to Lolo but decided not to shoot. Sincere was in charge, not Lolo.

"Clean this mess up," he ordered Lolo. Tyrell wiped his clothes off and walked quickly out of the shop. He sped back to the city in a daze.

When he got home, he fell out on the sofa.

Kanika ran to his side. "Your shirt and jeans—what is this?" she said, noticing the dark specks of blood on his sweats.

"I had to do it again."

"What?"

"Kill one of my own."

Kanika rubbed his face. "Who was it this time?"

"Sincere. They didn't get rid of Mike. Mike is still alive."

"Hell no!" Kanika said. "Then he deserved to be bodied."

"True, but with Mike and Sincere gone, I need someone I can trust."

"Exactly. You shouldn't be having to do all of this. You need a real lieutenant who can look after these niggas for you and body them if he has to. You need a right hand."

"I just feel like there's no one," Tyrell said.

Kanika thought for a few seconds. "I know just the person: Big Gee."

"You mean Big Gee who used to run with me and Tony?" Tyrell's eyes started to brighten.

"Yes. I speak to Sheila all the time, and they can use the money. Even though he said he was tired of the game and he was too old, he'll do it for the right price. He's the only one I trust. He'll do it for me."

*G*irl, *I* am so nervous about this," Sheila said. She and Kanika had talked about her husband, Big Gee, joining Tyrell. "Y'all gonna have to talk to Big Gee directly."

"We will, but I wanted to feel you out on this." Kanika gazed at Little T in Sheila's arms. "We can use his help."

"Trust me, I am sure he'll do it, and I want him to. We need the money. But we just started to have a quiet little life."

"Well, that's what I thought, too."

She and Sheila laughed. "But of course, girl, I will always be there for the both of you. Besides, how you and Tyrell doing in general? How's the new apartment?"

"It's nice, comfortable, with excellent security. It ain't Brooklyn, though."

"Ain't you ever gonna be happy?" Sheila asked as she hopped Little T up and down on her lap.

"I don't know," Kanika said, resting her chin on her hand. "Not until this whole thing with Tiffany is settled. That girl will not rest until I am dead. How can I be happy knowing that?"

"But you gotta live your life. Don't let no trick-ass bitch keep you down. You come from royalty, girl." Sheila smiled. "With you and Tyrell in this together, can't nobody fuck with that."

Kanika handed Sheila a bottle to feed Little T. "How did you and Big Gee do it?"

"We didn't have a choice. Once it was over with Tony, he was gone."

"But why didn't he reach out to Tyrell?"

"You know how men are. I think everyone was just kind of shocked how everything happened. It shook us all up. I think Big Gee thought Tyrell had it all under control."

"Well, he does—"

"Come on, girl, be honest. The game is changing. Honor and keeping your word doesn't mean the same thing anymore. Everybody is about doing them. It's about the individual. That's not how you succeed in the life we live."

"I was thinking that, too. When I was growing up, I had no idea what my mommy and Tony did until I was much older. Everything was so secretive."

"These days, everybody wanna get rich, and if they can't, it's over for them," Sheila said, holding Little T as she fed him. "Big Gee probably thought Tyrell was out for self."

"Tyrell has never been like that. He just had to look out for all of us, and unfortunately, the wrong people got caught up in it."

Sheila nodded.

"But besides that, I love him. I know he's doing his best. Sometimes I wonder, though, how long can we keep this up? What's it gonna be like for Little T when he grows up?"

"If y'all make enough money, maybe you two won't have to explain shit to anybody. Little T will just think his parents are 'entrepreneurs.'"

"I don't think so. When I found out, I still didn't know what it meant. Little T will know. All the images and the videos and the rap songs talk about our life. What if he wants to be down with that?"

"And he ain't?"

"I don't want him to. Though I'm in it, I fell in love with the man, not the drug game. You know I always wanted to be regular."

"You could never be regular even if you tried. You always shined, Kanika."

"Thank you." Kanika smiled. "But I want our son to have that chance to be regular if he wants to. We ain't the Mafia. I don't want him following Tyrell."

"What does Tyrell say?"

"We never really talked about that. But he'll do what I say. I want our son to be a doctor, lawyer, or a legitimate business owner," Kanika boasted.

"Everything you wasn't, right?"

"Right."

Two days later, Kanika and Tyrell drove to Jersey City to visit Big Gee and Sheila. As Kanika sat in the car, she prayed that everything would go well.

At Big Gee's house, Kanika and Sheila attended to the children while Tyrell and Big Gee talked. But both women kept a close eye on their men.

"It's mad good to see you and your fam, man," Big Gee said as he passed a cigar to Tyrell.

"Took us a while to get here, but this was all Kanika's idea. I should've thought of it." Tyrell laughed.

"They say behind a great man, there's a great woman," Big Gee said.

Tyrell dangled the cigar between his fingers. "She ain't behind me, man. She's right next to a nigga."

"Even better. I gotta admit, though, I was waiting for this day when we can talk business." Big Gee leaned in and lit their cigars.

"I understand that you left the game for whatever reasons, but we need to discuss that," Tyrell said.

"To be honest, I wasn't really feeling how everything went down and how you did Tony and 'em. But after a while, after I looked at all the facts, I knew that it had to be done. Tony was from the old school."

"Sometimes old school is good."

"Yeah, but he was way too laid-back for the young cats that was coming up. We needed some new blood. And you that blood."

"I need a true right-hand man. Who can look out for me and mine. I don't wanna be dealing with niggas. I wanna spend more time with my family. Chill in the cut."

"That's what you should be doing. That's what Tony did 'cause he had you."

"Well, ain't too many of me left these days."

"I can do what you need. In fact, it's all I know. Sheila got me around here doing lawn work and shit. Man, I wanna have these hands over somebody's neck, not a damn lawn mower," Big Gee blew small circles of smoke out his mouth.

"Gimme the lawn mower, man." Tyrell laughed. "Since Kanika and I got married, it's been drama after drama. Not that drama ends, but I wanna be able to know someone else can take care of it."

Big Gee simply listened.

"So, you down?"

"I wanna be down, but not sure if I can."

Tyrell looked at Kanika, who was nearby.

"You know I got a family to feed, man," Big Gee said.

Kanika handed Tyrell an envelope. Tyrell handed it to Big Gee. "Can this help?"

Big Gee stuck the cigar in his mouth. When he looked at the amount of money in the envelope, he nearly burned himself when the cigar dropped out. "Sheila," Big Gee shouted, "get yourself another motherfuckin' lawn mower!"

Everyone laughed. Big Gee and Tyrell shook hands.

Chapter 10

Tiffany **was at the** top of her game now. With Lexus helping her run the streets, she had more free time than she knew what to do with. It was perfect, she thought. Now, she could focus even more on her efforts for payback.

She had plans to return to New York this weekend. This time, they were headed to Brooklyn. Word was that Tyrell had set up shop there and she had every reason to do the same. Rasheeda hooked her up with one of her old friends who had a crib in East New York. Tiffany planned to chill there and run her VA business over the phone for a while. She had cut her hair and changed its color to a bleached blond. She wanted to look completely different, completely unrecognizable. Lexus was supposed to join her in a few days because he knew Tyrell personally from back in the day. Mike couldn't be seen alive in Brooklyn, so she hooked him up with a place in VA and a spot on her team as a lookout. But Tiffany and Lexus were ready to swoop down on Kanika and Tyrell's son and take him back to VA. All Tiffany needed to do was find out exactly where Kanika and the baby were.

"Don't worry about a thing when you're gone," Rasheeda said, helping Tiffany pack the white Range Rover Rasheeda had bought

for her a few months back. "You a top bitch now. You got under-
lings doing the work for you. So you handle yours without stress."

"I'm glad I got Lexus out there. I know he will keep niggas in
check. I don't play when it comes to my money."

"Our money." Rasheeda grinned as she patted Tiffany on her
ass.

They both hadn't mentioned what had happened a few nights
ago. It was as if nothing happened, but for Tiffany *everything* happened that night.

"Make sure you tell Nikki. I will check for her soon," Rasheeda
said as Tiffany got in the backseat.

Tiffany slipped on her shades. "Oh, I will. But you know this is
not a vacation. I am coming back with a baby. You didn't forget,
did you?"

"Hell I didn't. I don't want no snot-nose kid around. I mean,
exactly what you expect to do with the baby when you get back?"

"Bring Kanika and Tyrell to their knees. Before I know it, I'll
have everything from VA to New York. Shit, they may not even get
that fuckin' baby back."

"I got you hooked up with a small place to stay. You need to
be in the hood and not up in a fancy hotel getting massages."

Tiffany laughed. "That's cool. I didn't want to, anyway. I want
to be as close to Tyrell as possible." She hugged Rasheeda good-
bye and instructed the driver to take her to the airport. Lexus
was arriving on a later plane. Tiffany examined her first-class
tickets—she would be in New York in just a few hours.

At around midafternoon, Tiffany pulled up to Nikki's building. It was exactly what she had prayed it wasn't—a far cry
from her luxurious surroundings with Rasheeda—but it had to

do. This is what she wanted. There were a gang of teens in front of the building, sneakers hanging from tree branches, and empty cartons of Chinese food skipping down the street from the wind. When she stepped out the black Escalade, all heads turned to her. But as soon as Nikki came outside, everyone seemed to go back to their business.

"Hey, are you Tiffany?" Nikki asked, dressed in jeans and a cut-off white tee and a black head kerchief. "I'm Nikki."

"Nice to meet you. Can we go upstairs?" Tiffany asked as she handed Nikki her bags. Tiffany kept her shades on and wanted to disappear inside as fast as possible.

Nikki's apartment was only a three-bedroom, with gray carpet and yellow walls. Tiffany wondered why she hadn't gotten a hotel room, but Rasheeda convinced her that she needed to blend into Brooklyn life. Besides, she thought, all she needed was a few days to get her business done.

"I know you're used to Rasheeda's fat crib, but I hope this will do," Nikki said as she and Tiffany walked around.

Tiffany spun around on her heels. "It'll do. I just need a place to sleep because I'm basically gonna be out most of the time."

Nikki walked to the kitchen and came back with two bottles of Gatorade. "Thirsty?"

Tiffany put down her Gucci bag and took the drink. As she sipped, she wondered how this simple girl knew someone like Rasheeda. Nikki didn't seem that hood at all. But when Nikki turned around, Tiffany saw a long line of tattoos going from the nape of her neck disappearing down her back.

"So, make yourself at home, and if there is anything I can do—"

Tiffany thought for a moment as she savored the sweet, cold drink. "Do you know why I'm here?"

"I don't think that's any of my business."

"Well, it is because I am in your house. I am here to take what's mine from someone who took everything from me."

"Rasheeda may have mentioned something like that," Nikki said, looking away from Tiffany like she wanted to avoid the conversation.

"So, I may need your help."

Nikki looked at Tiffany. "I can help you with directions or give you the inside scoop. I don't do guns and I don't do blood."

Tiffany sported a fat grin. "How the hell do you know Rasheeda?"

Nikki laughed lightly. "My mother and her aunt were friends. When I was at Hampton, I stayed with Rasheeda for the first summer. My mom had her new man and didn't want me coming back up to New York. So, we got cool—"

"How cool?"

Nikki looked at Tiffany like she was crazy. "She was nice. She looked out."

Tiffany nodded. She couldn't assume that every woman Rasheeda knew was a lover. She had a feeling that Nikki was indeed just a friend. "Did she tell you about Kanika and Tyrell?"

That seemed to catch Nikki's attention as her eyes narrowed in on Tiffany's face. "She did, but everyone knows Tyrell around here. He's like the fucking King of Brooklyn. New York is more like it."

Tiffany rolled her eyes. "You know where he stay with his bitch?"

"Nah. But we can roll by his barbershop—"

"I don't want people to see me. I wanna lay low."

"So, how you expect to get what you want?"

"All I need to do is find out where he lives."

"That I don't know," Nikki said, shaking her head.

"Oh, but you *will* find out."

The next day, Tiffany and Nikki drove down to Tyrell's barbershop in Brooklyn. Tiffany waited in the car while Nikki went in and did her thing. Already, Tiffany was taken by what she saw from the outside. The shop had a gold-and-gray silver awning and lit up the rather dirty Fulton Street block. The inside looked even nicer, with a wide-screen television and oak décor she could see from the outside.

"Excuse me," Nikki said as she walked inside. "Anybody know where I can find Tyrell?"

Several of the barbers looked at each other. No one wanted to answer directly.

"Who you?" asked an older man, about five-eight, wearing a black barber cloak. He sized Nikki up, but softened his approach as soon as she turned around. Nikki had on fitted jeans, with a white halter top and shiny pink lipstick that accentuated her light skin and pouty mouth.

"I'm just a *friend*," Nikki said with a sly smile. The men looked at each other like they knew what that meant.

"Well, he ain't in today," said another dude who was about six-five with a round belly. He walked up to Nikki. "Something you need?"

Nikki held her breath at the behemoth of a man. He didn't look at all like he had time for bullshit. "I was just wondering—"

Then Tyrell walked up from downstairs. "Yo, I'll check you later," Tyrell shouted as he exited from the back of the store.

By the way the others acknowledged him, Nikki knew that was him. "Never mind," she said, running outside to the truck.

"That's him, that's him," Nikki squealed as she and Tiffany scooted down in their seats. Tiffany peered out the window a bit. Her eyes couldn't come off Tyrell. She thought he looked even better than the last time she saw him. Dark, tall, smooth with a swagger as he slipped into his shiny Benz coupe.

"Did you find out where he live?" Tiffany asked.

"They didn't tell me."

"Just drive," Tiffany huffed. "We have to follow him wherever he goes."

After several stops and detours, they ended up in Manhattan an hour and a half later, making sure they stayed several cars behind the Benz.

Tyrell pulled up to his building on East Thirty-eighth, and a valet took his car keys.

Tiffany and Nikki waited across the street and watched.

"Damn, girl, you should just go in the building with him. I need to find out what floor he on," Tiffany said, practically pushing Nikki out of the car.

Nikki ran across the street to catch Tyrell going in. There was a burly security guard whom Tyrell shared a few words with. When they were done, Nikki slipped in like she was with him by giving him the guard a wink. The guard looked confused but let her go.

"Hold the elevator!" Nikki shouted, as she slid inside the closing doors. "Hi," she said, her breathing fast and heavy.

Tyrell smirked at her. "I know you?"

"No, I'm just, uhm, visiting someone," Nikki said. "I'm an exchange student from NYU."

Tyrell simply nodded as he stared at the numbers in the elevator going higher and higher.

Nikki glanced at him several times, hoping to catch his eye, but his mind seemed thousands of miles away. When they got to the eighteenth floor, he got off without a word.

Nikki stuck her head out to see which direction he walked in, but he cut the corner too fast.

When Nikki came back out, Tiffany was standing outside the car. "Girl, that took forever. What happened?"

"He lives on the eighteenth floor, but I didn't get the apartment number," Nikki said, getting in the car.

"Did he see you?"

"Yes." Nikki smiled like that was a good thing.

"Look, if he saw you and got off at the eighteenth floor, that means the nigga don't live on the eighteenth floor. Tyrell is a smart muthafucka. I'm just gonna have to find out myself."

Chapter 11

Kanika lay on the bed with Little Tyrell on her chest. He had his mother's sleepy bedroom eyes. But everything else was Tyrell's, from his nose to the way his belly button stuck out. She wanted her son to grow to have a normal life, though it might never happen. She thought her mother must have had the same thoughts about her, but here she was living the life, three generations deep.

"How my people doin'?" Tyrell asked when he walked into the bedroom and plopped down beside Kanika and the baby.

"Why you so out of breath?" Kanika asked, handing him Little Tyrell.

"I had to walk up ten flights of steps." Tyrell hopped his son up and down on his chest as Little Tyrell smiled away.

"Why the hell you did that?"

"Some bitch was on the elevator with me. I didn't know who the fuck she was. So, I cut out early in case she was—"

"Was what? This is a good building. We can't keep being so paranoid like this."

Tyrell looked at her strange. "Did you forget what happened with me and Mike? Did you forget he tried to kill me?"

Kanika didn't say a word. He was right, she thought. They always had to watch their backs, no matter what.

Tyrell laid the baby on his chest. Little Tyrell dozed off in the silence.

"So, who was that girl, you think?" Kanika asked after some time.

"I don't know. Maybe some chick who knows one of the nannies or something. I just ain't taking no chances."

"Is that why you keep the apartment in Brooklyn still?"

Tyrell studied Kanika's face. "Why you ask me that?"

Kanika picked up the annoyance in his tone. She didn't like that at all. "Because we are married and we have two homes. Why you need one all to yourself?"

Tyrell put the baby in his crib. His shoulders touched Kanika's as he sat beside her. "You don't trust me?"

Kanika moved a few inches away. "Should I?"

Tyrell moved closer. He put his arm around her shoulder. "Do you ever think I'd cheat on you? For real."

Kanika sat without moving and looked in his eyes. His handsome face with the smooth black skin and brown eyes would make any woman drop her panties, she thought. "No, not really."

Tyrell kissed her glossed raisin-colored lips. "I'll always be loyal. Until death do us part."

"We talking about *cheating*," she corrected.

"That's the same thing as being loyal."

"No, it ain't. Don't fuck with me, Tyrell."

Tyrell smirked as he kept his arms around her. "Well, ain't it good I kept it so Big Gee and his family can have a place to stay?"

Kanika didn't answer.

"Besides, why we even talking about this. It ain't mine no more," he said. "Why you beefing?"

"Because I would've never known. I swear, Tyrell, if I ever find out you even thinking of messing with somebody else, I'll destroy you," Kanika said in an icy tone.

Tyrell let out a heavy breath. "So, just because I came up through your family you think you can destroy *me*?"

Kanika stood up and faced him. "Just because I had your baby and I'm a mother now doesn't mean I can't get down if I have to. Just don't test me. Understand?"

Tyrell clenched his jaw tightly. "Yeah, I understand," he said through his teeth, and walked out of the room.

That Friday, Dre, one of Tyrell's boys at the barbershop, was throwing a birthday party at the Tunnel in Manhattan. It was one of those parties everyone knew about but only few could actually get into. When Kanika and Tyrell arrived, limos and the latest model Benzes and Infinitis lined the block. It was chaotic.

When Kanika and Tyrell got inside, the party really began. It was all courtesy of Tyrell, as he bought out the club and shut it down for his boy. Dre was one of the dudes he had come up with, who was just released on parole. The party was not just a celebration of Dre's birthday, but also of his relative freedom. But Tyrell would never consider putting Dre back on his team. He had been out of the game too long.

Kanika couldn't stop moving her body to the music. It had been a while since she and Tyrell had hung out like this. The baby was with a nanny, so Kanika had no worries tonight. She felt especially sexy in a short, skimpy black-and-gold Versace dress that accentuated her thighs and ass. Her gold jewels shimmered under the lights as did her shiny, black long hair and dark brown flawless skin. Tyrell was dressed in black, too, in Armani slacks and a buttoned shirt. They wore matching gold chains with pendants of a lion and a lioness. That's exactly how it was between the two of them. Kanika just hoped they'd never have to bite each other.

"You guys look so damn good together," said Sheila. "Tyrell, how you get so lucky to get a beautiful girl like Kanika?"

Kanika laughed. "That's right, remind him."

Tyrell wrapped his arms around her from behind. "I ain't got to be reminded. After Kanika pursued me nonstop, I finally gave in to her."

Kanika laughed harder. "He's half right. You know how these niggas get when they get some bread."

"True, true." Sheila grinned. "You two are like the king and queen up in here." Sheila looked around at their table with the bottles of Cristal and Moët. "I have to thank you guys for doing this for Dre."

"That's my boy. He's been down forever. Now, he working and—"

"I can't afford to lose my baby again." Sheila's eyes got watery. "I just need him to walk a straight line. I'll talk to you two later." She smiled and walked away.

Kanika moved her shoulders to the music as she backed her behind on Tyrell, who was up against the wall.

Several people came by their section to give them their pounds and respect. But it wasn't until Big Gee came through that Tyrell loosened up some more.

Kanika chilled with Sheila, Denise, and a few of the other girlfriends as they danced to the latest Jay-Z joint. The club was hot, the champagne was flowing, and the music was banging. Kanika and Denise even got into a little dance-off with old-school moves when an MC Lyte song came on.

After a few songs, Kanika stood up on the table and did her

best wind-up dance to the reggae song that played. Tyrell watched
her from below and egged her on. She was good, and she was a
little tipsy when a few of the other girls joined her on the table.
Then Tyrell took her by her hand, brought her down, and they
danced together for what seemed like the whole night, tonguing
each other down and feeling each other's bodies. When the song
changed, Tyrell dragged her upstairs to the unisex bathroom.

Kanika and Tyrell slipped inside the crowded bathroom and
had a stall all to themselves at the end. He lifted her panties with
one hand and took out his dick with the other. Kanika put her leg
up on the toilet seat and bent over, while Tyrell slipped in from
behind. She held the wall in front of her as he gripped her hips,
pushing deeper inside her. The loud music drowned out her wails
of pleasure as Tyrell made her come. They stood up and kissed
until someone knocked on the stall to use it. Kanika and Tyrell
walked out like nothing happened. A few people winked at them,
knowing what time it was. It wasn't like nobody else was doing it,
Kanika thought. The club was notorious for its bathroom tales.

Kanika stayed behind to freshen up in the mirror. Her skin
was glowing, she thought, as she applied a fresh coat of cranberry
red lipstick. She dabbed her skin with a cool wet towel while a few
jealous females looked on.

When she walked out and down the steps to the end of the
club where Tyrell was, she caught the eyes of a blond-haired female across the room. The girl kept her eyes fixated on Kanika's
every step. Kanika stopped, put her hand on her hip, and stared
in the girl's direction. The girl made a sarcastic smirk and turned
to talk to another girl seated next to her wearing a head kerchief.
Kanika kept walking, but couldn't take the blond-haired girl's
face out of her mind the rest of the night.

———

G **et up,**" Tyrell said, gently nudging Kanika awake. Tired and groggy, she looked at the clock. It was 9 A.M. They had gotten home only three hours ago. "What happened?" she asked in a throaty voice. Tyrell had the baby in one hand and a bag in another. They were both fully dressed.

"I wanna show you something," he said, flashing a grin.

Kanika rubbed the sleep out of her eyes. Tyrell was always an early riser. She wondered if he even slept sometimes, with all the stuff he had on his mind. "Where are we going so early?"

"Just get dressed." He threw a pair of sweatpants and a T-shirt at her. "It's a surprise."

Kanika slipped on the clothes, brushed her teeth, and before she knew it, she was in the car riding to Brooklyn.

"What is it?" she asked, her eyes looking away from the bright June sun that peered into the car.

"Well, I was thinking that maybe you been home for too long. You know what you said about destroying me?"

Kanika cut her eyes at him. "Yes?"

"You feel you need to prove something since you been holed up in the house with a baby—"

"That is not true," Kanika said, shaking her head, but she had been feeling really helpless lately. "Well, not one hundred percent true."

"Okay, whatever."

"I did mean what I said." Kanika kept her tone firm. "I've just been real tired lately. I don't think I could handle anything else without fucking cracking up."

Tyrell stayed silent as he drove the car over the Brooklyn Bridge and up Fulton Street. Not too long after, they were pulling up at the barbershop.

"Why did you bring us here? It look like they are fine without you," Kanika said as she noticed the barbershop was up and running already. She took the baby out of the car and into her arms.

"We ain't here for the barbershop. We here for you," he said, pulling out some keys.

Kanika slipped on her Chanel shades. She had no idea what Tyrell was up to as he attempted to unlock the shut-down store next door. He pulled up the metal barricade.

"You ready?" Tyrell asked, and opened the door.

Kanika walked into the space and nearly fell on the floor. It was a lavishly decorated brand-new spa with her name scrolled in gold on the inside: *Kanika's.*

"Oh my God," Kanika said, handing the baby to Tyrell as she ran through the spa, touching the yellow and pink leather chairs, fresh orchid arrangements, and examining the wide-plank black-stained wood floors. It looked like something out of one of her dreams.

"Thank you." She wrapped her arms around Tyrell. "So what do I do with this?"

"It's all yours. I wanna see you happy and use those smarts you have to make us another million." He smiled. "You can hire a manager and basically collect the money. You can make it whatever you want. You can hire and fire whoever you want. The first spa in the hood."

Kanika touched her chest. "I can think of so many things I'd want to do with this. I can add a little girls' spa day for the mothers to bring their daughters. I need the best nail stylists in here and eyebrow people—"

Tyrell listened as Kanika walked around the salon mentally noting everything she could do to make the place its best.

"You think Sheila is interested?" Kanika asked.

"She did manage Lulu's Salon for a while," Tyrell said.

"Cool," Kanika said. "I am too excited!"

"What's the best part?" he asked, drawing her close to him.

She put her hand on her baby's head and on Tyrell's face. "Working next to you," she said. "You don't even know what you started."

Chapter 12

Tiffany and Lexus spent the night in a car across the street from Tyrell's building. They saw Tyrell and Kanika leave in the morning without the baby. Tiffany assumed the baby was with a babysitter or not at home. She had no time to find out, because this was her last day in New York and she had to do what she came here for.

Tiffany noticed how happy Kanika looked this morning, leaving arm in arm with Tyrell. She twisted her face in disgust at the thought of how happy they could be, but smiled when she thought about the drama she was about to unleash.

"You ready?" asked Lexus, who stuffed two loaded 9's in his holster. Tiffany had a small 2-millimeter. They weren't sure what to expect once they got upstairs, but didn't want any surprises.

They were both dressed in business suits to appear as no threat. Tiffany had the script all planned out. She was nervous, but she didn't show it.

They walked across the street to the building. It was only 9 A.M., but people were still trickling out the front doors on their way to work or morning errands. Tiffany hoped the man at the security desk would be distracted, but when they walked in, he was at full attention.

"Good morning. Can I help you?" asked the young, thirtyish Latino with a mustache.

"Yes, we're here for Tyrell and Kanika Johnson," Tiffany said, putting on her professional voice. Her black wig was itching her, but she avoided scratching it.

"Sure, but they left for the day already—"

"We know, but they said we can leave something upstairs for them," Lexus added as he stood by, holding a briefcase.

"Hold on, let me see." The security attendant called upstairs and spoke into the intercom.

Tiffany and Lexus smiled when they heard a woman's voice.

"Okay, the nanny says they are not expecting anyone. Sorry."

Tiffany clenched her jaw. "Okay, well, thank you," she said, marching out of the building with Lexus trailing behind her.

"Why the fuck you did that?" he said when they hopped in the car.

Tiffany slammed her passenger door. "I didn't want to cause a scene with that guard. We'll just sit out here and wait till the nanny comes down. She gotta take the baby out at some point."

"But we need to be done with this today," Lexus said, loosening his tie.

Tiffany couldn't help but notice how sexy he looked in a suit. It draped his muscular body perfectly. "We will," she said, glancing at the loosened button on his white shirt. "We just gotta wait. When she come out, we just pounce on that bitch and take the baby. We'll be on the plane by tonight."

Like a focused, still owl on a branch, Tiffany waited five hours in the car. To avoid using the bathroom, she didn't eat or drink. When she saw a nanny come out with a baby in the stroller, she pushed Lexus awake.

"Get ready, nigga."

Tiffany jumped out of the car and walked calmly across the street. "Excuse me," she said to the nanny, an older Asian woman. "Do you know if Tyrell is home?" That was her test to see if she had the right baby.

"No, he at work," the nanny said with a confused look on her face as she stopped the baby carriage.

"Is this his son? Oh my God, he's as beautiful as he said he was," Tiffany lied as she touched the baby's hand. The infant immediately grabbed hers. The baby giggled at her, and she had a sudden pang of guilt. This was her little nephew, she thought.

"You family?" asked the nanny.

"Yes," Tiffany said. "Can I hold the baby?"

"No, we must go," said the nanny as she pushed the carriage forward. Tiffany stood in front of her.

"Bitch, give her the baby," Lexus said, sticking the gun to the nanny, who jumped at the pressure at her back.

Tiffany jumped, too. There was a look of horror in the nanny's eyes. But at that instant, Tiffany saw the nanny press a button on the carriage and push it full force into Tiffany, causing her to fall. Lexus's gun went off into the nanny's back. The security guard ran outside, and Lexus shot in his direction but missed.

Tiffany tried to grab the baby, but a stranger had run up and whisked away the carriage. Next thing she heard were police sirens. She and Lexus ran into the car, leaving behind a scene that was already crawling with people standing over the nanny's blood-covered body.

Lexus sped off while Tiffany banged on the window in frustration. She had never wanted anyone to get killed—shot maybe, but not dead. At least not yet. She saw a young white lady holding the baby in her arms and pointing down the street. This just wasn't going to work, she thought. But she did have one final idea.

O**n the** plane ride back to Virginia, Tiffany was numb. She replayed the scene a thousand times in her head. There were a million things they could've done, she thought.

"That dumb bitch should've just given you the baby," Lexus said, frustrated. "Dumb bitch is a dead bitch."

"Whatever. We fucked up. Why didn't you just knock her down or something?"

"Yo, I did what I had to do."

Tiffany understood. "What was that button she pressed?" Tiffany asked, as they sat in first class.

"Some security shit. You never seen those? It's like an alarm that you press and it signals to the parents that the baby is in danger. It also tracks the baby and wherever the carriage goes."

Tiffany looked at him sideways. She held in her laugh. "How the hell you know that?"

"My boy had one for his kid. It got pressed one day when his baby mama was out with the baby and got sick. He got the message right there and tracked down where she was."

"Shit," Tiffany said, and rubbed her forehead with both hands. "That nigga got every kind of security shit. The hell with kidnapping that fuckin' baby. He probably already know."

"Just let me cap that nigga."

"Too easy," said Tiffany. "But I'm working on something."

"But you looked good in that suit," Lexus said, his eyes turning deep and low.

"You did, too," said Tiffany, smiling. "Don't let me have to fuck you."

Lexus laughed so hard, the people in front of them turned around. "Like I said, your wish is my command."

Tiffany walked in the house about 2 A.M. The first thing she smelled was weed smoke. She followed the scent down to the basement to Rasheeda's office. The door was half-opened, and Rasheeda was seated at her desk amongst stacks of money and plastic bags of coke. Tiffany barely saw her behind the smoky haze of weed.

"Rasheeda?" Tiffany asked, closing the door behind her. "What you doing?"

Rasheeda spun her chair around and puffed out small circles. "Where's the baby?" she asked, stern-faced.

Tiffany sat down across from her. There were small specks of white dust under Rasheeda's nose, but she didn't dare mention it. "It's a long story."

Rasheeda flashed a smile as she sipped from a near-finished glass of Henny. "I got all night."

"We messed up," Tiffany said, rubbing the back of her neck. "It didn't work."

Rasheeda's face screwed up in shock. "Are you fucking crazy? You sit here and act like it ain't no big thing."

"It ain't. The baby is fine. The nanny is dead. And we didn't hurt anybody else. We had everything planned down to the second," Tiffany said in an anxious tone. She was getting the feeling that Rasheeda was more than angry.

"Bitch! You can't be going around fucking shit up, killing niggas, and talking about you messed up! All that's gonna do is bring all the attention on me. On us!"

Tiffany froze.

Rasheeda's forehead broke out in beads of sweat. "How could

you go up to New York and kill a fucking nanny and still ain't get the business done!"

Tiffany covered her hands with her face. "Lexus—"

"Lexus works for you," Rasheeda said, pointing in Tiffany's face so close, her finger grazed Tiffany's nose. "That nigga can't do nothing unless you tell him. Or were you just too focused on the dick between his legs?"

"It's not our fault! We did everything. The nigga Tyrell got some wild-ass security shit going on—"

"Fuck it!" Rasheeda said, standing over Tiffany. "By now, them niggas know what happened. All hell is gonna break loose on your ass. You ready to lay it down? Even your life?"

Chapter 13

Kanika held her little Tyrell in her arms like it was the first time. She didn't want to let him go. She stared out the window, rocking him in her arms and looking at the taped-off murder scene down below. *That could've been my baby.* The tears in her eyes streamed down her face. She didn't even bother drying them anymore.

"Everything is gonna be all right. I know who is behind this without question," Tyrell said, stuffing the cell phone in his pocket. He had been on it all afternoon.

"I do, too," Kanika said, her throat dry and painful from the hard crying she did earlier. "It's so sad what happened to Ms. Chin. She got to this country, and she gotta meet us."

"Listen," Tyrell said, holding her from behind. "We didn't do anything wrong."

"It was Tiffany, I know," Kanika said, carrying the baby to the crib. "I swear I'm gonna kill that bitch. Gimme the phone."

"Why?"

"Gimme the phone!" Kanika said.

"Yo, we hot right now. The cops is asking everyone in the building questions. I gotta take care of this my way."

"Call Big Gee—" Kanika handed him back the phone. "I wanna talk to him."

Tyrell dialed Big Gee's number. "Yo, man, Kanika need something."

Kanika grabbed the phone. "I need you to find Tiffany and her fucking crew. Them niggas did this. I want that bitch done! Then I wanna see the body." Kanika waited for Big Gee's response. She stared at Tyrell, who rolled his eyes away. "Well?" she asked him.

"Tyrell already gave me those orders. But I'll let you see the body. Which part you want?"

"Everything," Kanika said, and hung up.

"Did you have to do that?" Tyrell asked. "I told you I am handling this."

"Handling what! Look at what almost happened to our son. Nothing is being handled until now!"

Tyrell stepped to Kanika so close, she flinched. "Yo, lower your fucking voice. Are you saying I ain't doing enough?"

Kanika folded her arms across her chest. "We need to work together on this, Tyrell. This bitch need to be brought down, like today. Now!" Kanika huffed as she opened the closet in the hallway. "As a matter of fact, I am going there myself." She pulled out a suitcase and dropped any piece of clothing she could find as she cried hysterically.

"Chill, chill," Tyrell said, trying to hold her back as she tried to kick and scream out of his grip.

"Get off me!" she cried. "My mother would never stand for this. I can't stay here and let this happen. Somebody told him where we live, too. I'ma find out!"

"Yo, chill!" Tyrell said. He grabbed her by her shoulders and pushed her against the wall.

The impact of the wall surprised Kanika, and she crumbled down to her knees and caught her breath. "I am so scared, Tyrell."

Tyrell wrapped her completely in his arms. "I know, boo. I got you. Just let me do what I do. Just let me," Tyrell said as he rocked Kanika in his arms.

The following day at the spa, Kanika had gone in to just let everyone know she was doing okay. She brought her son with her and explained what happened at least ten times to anyone who asked.

"Girl, I swear if anything had happened to you or that baby . . . we all would've been down there in Virgina for real," Sheila said as she led one of the spa's clients to a chair to get her done by Denise.

"What makes y'all think the only problem is in Virginia?" Denise chimed in. She was working at the spa now as a stylist. "Them niggas had to know where to go. How the hell they gonna know where Kanika and Tyrell live?"

"Well," Kanika said, bouncing the baby on her lap, "Tyrell said there was some chick in the elevator one day that looked like she was following him."

Denise twisted her mouth. "My point exactly."

Sheila tucked her short cropped hair behind her ears. "You know, I did see a chick come in the barbershop when I was dropping off something to Dre a couple of weeks ago. She was asking for Tyrell. She looked familiar, though."

Kanika raised her eyebrows. "Who was that?"

"I know I had seen her before somewhere," Sheila said, snapping her fingers. "I can find out."

"Please do," Kanika said. "Because if I find out some bitch up here set me up, I'm getting in that ass. Oooh!" Kanika bit down on her teeth. "I can't wait to find out!"

Two **days** later, Tyrell waited in his office until he heard from Big Gee. Things had been real quiet. He didn't want to go home without telling Kanika something.

Then his phone rang. "Whatsup."

"You gonna be happy about this," Big Gee said with a smile in his voice.

"Ain't nothing can make me happy right now, man."

"We got Mike. Nigga was holed up in some little shack down in Virginia. He was the one who told niggas where to go."

"Told who?"

"Tiffany and some dude Lexus. Then they got this other bitch, Rasheeda, behind it all."

"And Mike?"

"Dead as muthafuckin' wood. Nigga had the nerve to beg."

"Anyway, one down, more to go. You know where this bitch Rasheeda stay?"

"We got all of that. Gimme a day or two. I'll get back at you—"

"You my man, Gee. These niggas don't know what they started."

Tyrell knew things were only going to get worse, not better. As he drove back to the city, he realized he and Kanika had to make some major changes that would spare their lives.

When he walked in their apartment, Kanika was cooking dinner while the baby played nearby.

"We gotta talk," he said while he watched her cut up some onions. "We need to talk about the baby."

Kanika wiped her hands with a towel. She caressed Tyrell's smooth face. "You look so tired, baby. I know you trying your best."

"Ain't nobody gonna hold us down. Understand?"

"I do," she said, and they kissed slow and hard.

He licked her taste from his lips. "Whatsup with that old lady that live near us back Upstate?"

Kanika shrugged. "She's real nice, like I told you. As a matter of fact, I've been meaning to visit her. I need to talk to someone who is living a normal life."

"Well, when you go, ask her if she'd want to take care of our little shorty. Little Tyrell can stay with her until we work this all out."

Kanika blew down hard. "You know, I was thinking the same thing. I just didn't wanna say anything—"

"It's the best thing. He can be in a calm environment, out of harm's way."

"And no nanny is gonna want to work for us after what happened. We'll have that black cloud over us."

"That's right," Tyrell said, opening the refrigerator for a beer. "Go see the old lady and see her right away. Bring Little Tyrell."

Kanika finished preparing dinner, her heart breaking. She didn't want to show Tyrell how much it hurt her to do what they'd decided. But she would kill herself if anything happened to her son just because she couldn't let go, even for a little while.

Chapter 14

Tiffany and Rasheeda were seated outside near the pool, waiting to hear from Lexus. They found out Mike was dead. His bullet-ridden body was found inside the apartment they had gotten for him. He was supposed to be the one who had the connects they needed to get closer to Tyrell. With no one to tell them what to do, and who to avoid, Lexus had to do the street work. They needed someone on their team from Tyrell's camp. That was the only way Tiffany thought she could get at him by his own hand.

Rasheeda eyed the security guards in front of her home. "I don't like this feeling I'm getting, Tiffany. Nothing has happened. When it's this quiet, it means niggas are plotting."

Tiffany crossed her legs and lay back on the cot. "Ain't no plot like the one I have in mind."

"What's that?" Rasheeda asked, turning her body to face Tiffany.

Tiffany adjusted the strap to her white bikini top. "I want to hurt Kanika. I wanna take what is closest to her. What she values more than anything."

"I'm listening," Rasheeda said, lighting a cigarette.

"I'm gonna fuck Tyrell. He's gonna be all mine," Tiffany said, slipping off her shades.

Rasheeda flicked the ashes of her cigarette on the ground as she smoked.

"So what you think?"

"If that's what you want to do, I'm cool with it. Just make sure you fuck him good," she said, waving her cigarette in the air.

"I'm gonna get him open. I may not be good at some things, but fucking is something I've had lots of practice with."

They smiled at each other. "How about I help you practice some new things?" Rasheeda ran her fingers up Tiffany's thighs.

The sounds of gunshots made them both drop to the ground.

"Stay down!" Rasheeda shouted to Tiffany, who ran for her gun a few feet away. As she got back, more shots came in their direction. Rasheeda got up to get her own piece, but she was shot in the leg and still managed to crawl inside.

Tiffany grabbed Rasheeda's gun from the table, ran to the balcony, and busted off at three men who ran up in Rasheeda's house.

Tiffany jumped over the balcony, opened the bunker behind the house, and ran to the basement. That was when she heard more shots and rummaged through Rasheeda's stash for the .22. But then everything stopped.

She heard nothing. She loaded and cocked her piece and walked up the steps. Her bikini bottom was chafing her, and she slipped it off. She didn't care. She was ready to catch a body anyhow. She crept up to the living room with only her bra on and saw three bodies lying on the floor, including Deyqwan's. She stepped over them when she saw Rasheeda sitting on the steps holding her bloody leg.

"Get me something!" Rasheeda said as blood streamed down her thighs.

Tiffany grabbed the tablecloth and wrapped it around Rasheeda's thigh. "Oh God! I can't stop this blood."

"Bitch, just tie it tight! Give it to me," Rasheeda said, tying it herself.

"Is the bullet still in there?" Tiffany said, wrapping a smaller cloth from the end table around her waist.

"I've gotten shot many times before. This just grazed me. Fuck!" she said as she limped up. "Look at my place. I got three dead niggas in the next room. Where's Lexus?"

"I'm right here," he said, walking in the living room with a 9 in one hand and his jeans torn. "I got all these niggas. Deyqwan got one until his boy shot Deyqwan in the back."

Tiffany shook her head in despair. This was one war she didn't want to fight on her own turf. She thought the sooner she could get back to New York, the better for everyone. Once she could control Tyrell, she'd be able to control everything else.

On **Saturday** night, Tiffany stayed home. Rasheeda was out at one of her territories in Memphis for the weekend. Lexus helped keep Tiffany secure and with company.

"Lexus, I gotta say that we are making at least a million dollars more a week with you on our team," Tiffany said, as she looked at the books. "I can't have niggas in New York trying to fuck that up for me."

"Them niggas is just jealous. Tyrell ain't pushing that kind of paper up there yet. He's still building his empire."

"I don't even wanna talk about that nigga right now. If my

daddy was alive, he would've been dead. But I'm glad he ain't. That way I can finish him."

"Yo, your daddy was the fuckin' man. I know he taught you well, and sometimes you gotta catch bees with honey. Know what I mean?"

Tiffany grinned. "Oh, I do."

"I'm talking about acting like you wanna call a truce then strike when niggas don't expect it."

"I don't know about that," Tiffany said. She looked Lexus up and down.

"What you know about, then?" Lexus asked in a tone that didn't mean business.

"I know that I like you. You like me?"

Lexus leaned back in the chair with his arms to his side. "Of course I do. How can I not? You fine as hell, bad as hell, I could only wonder."

Tiffany slipped her gun out of her holster and put it down on the desk. She sat on Lexus's lap and felt his hardness under her ass. "What if you didn't have to wonder anymore?"

Lexus met Tiffany's tongue with his. She unbuttoned his shirt and pants with ease. "I want you to fuck the shit out of me," Tiffany pleaded as he pulled her blouse over her head and unbuckled her bra.

Lexus laid her out on the desk and spread her legs open. He sucked on her pussy until she begged him to stop. She only hoped his dick game was as good as his tongue game. "I gotta have that dick inside me right now," she said, reaching down between his legs.

She grabbed his sweaty back as he pushed his way inside. Holding her ass, he brought her to the wall and barreled his weight into her. She thought they must've fucked like that for a good fifteen minutes until he brought her down to the floor. They did it in every imaginable position. She rode him until he called her name. This made her go even faster as she dug her eyes into his soul. She held him down and milked him of every bit of energy he had left. He came inside her but stayed hard.

He flipped Tiffany over and ate her ass out, getting it nice and wet.

"Put it in my ass," she said, getting on her knees.

Lexus wet his dick with his fingers and pushed it into her tightness.

"Oww, I love it when it hurts," she said as she pumped her ass against his dick.

Lexus fucked her so hard, she bumped her head several times against the wall, but that didn't stop her. Not until the door flew open.

"What the fuck?" Rasheeda busted into the room.

Tiffany and Lexus rushed around for their clothes.

"Get the fuck out!" Rasheeda said to Lexus as he put his clothes back on. But Lexus hesitated. "Nigga, if you don't—" Rasheeda aimed her gat at him.

Lexus cut his eyes at both Tiffany and Rasheeda and bounced.

Tiffany wanted to leave with him, but Rasheeda blocked the door.

"Excuse me," Tiffany said, trying to walk around her.

"Listen, you gutter bitch—" Rasheeda shoved Tiffany against the desk. "—you just gonna walk past me like I ain't shit?"

"You just busted in here like the muthafuckin' FBI!"

"This is my goddamn house. My damn office. And you my bitch," Rasheeda said with a mischievous grin. "Or did you forget?"

"Please," Tiffany said as she rolled her eyes. "I ain't nobody's bitch, especially no other female's!" Tiffany walked around Rasheeda again, but this time Rasheeda pulled her by her weave like a rag doll.

"I fuckin' made you into a head bitch. I gave you a place to live, money in your pocket, and fuckin' reign over this here game. And that's how you gonna be?"

Tiffany struggled to get her head out of Rasheeda's hold. Rasheeda held on to it tight enough that her roots began to swell and bleed in the front.

Finally Rasheeda let her go, and Tiffany backed up.

"I'm sorry," Tiffany said, covering her crying eyes. "I didn't mean for Lexus and me to go that far. He came on to me. I tried to stop him—"

"How can you fuck the *help*? You that desperate for dick?" Rasheeda said in a mocking tone. "You such a joke."

Tiffany felt awful. Her chest collapsed. She needed Rasheeda's approval more than anything. Rasheeda was the only person who really cared for her. "I'm sorry, Rasheeda. Please—" Tiffany took Rasheeda's arm.

"If you gonna be rollin' with me, it gotta be all about me—" Rasheeda had a satisfied look on her face.

Tiffany said quietly, "You didn't have a problem with me sleeping with Tyrell."

Rasheeda flared up again. "Because that nigga would never want you! You could never have him! Anybody with a fat ass can get Lexus. He ain't Tyrell."

Tiffany felt weak. Any confidence she had in herself over the last few months withered away. "Fine, I won't see Lexus anymore. I'll get rid of him."

"No, he is one of the top niggas right now. And we need him. He's an expert triggerman," Rasheeda said, turning calm suddenly. She wiped Tiffany's eyes. "But I need you, too."

Tiffany opened up under Rasheeda's touch. "So do I."

"I'm going to bed now, and I expect you there in ten minutes."

Ten minutes later, Tiffany dried her eyes, lay down beside Rasheeda, and fell asleep in her arms.

Chapter 15

The following week, Kanika was at the spa while Tyrell was home with Little T. All the chairs were filled with clients, and everything was looking good. She had implemented a few new services like after-work pedicure specials that promised to get clients out with dried, pretty toenails in under thirty minutes. She had women of all colors from all over Brooklyn coming to her spa. She couldn't wait to start working on a self-improvement and pampering program for the younger girls who lived on the rough block where the spa was located.

During lunch, Kanika decided she might as well go home. Her mind was still concerned not only about Little T, but Tyrell, too. She felt she needed to be there for her family.

"Kanika, before you go, you gotta come with me to Denise's place," Sheila said with worried eyes. "There's somebody you need to see."

"Who?"

Sheila grabbed her car keys, and Kanika followed her out the door. "You found out who that bitch was who helped Tiffany."

"And then some," Sheila said.

They drove about five minutes to Denise's crib. Kanika could hardly wait to get out of the car.

When they walked in the apartment, Nikki was tied to a chair as Denise stood by, patiently filing her nails.

"This bitch made me late for work," Denise said, kicking Nikki's chair.

Nikki shook in her seat. "I swear I didn't—"

Kanika slapped Nikki across her mouth hard enough to bust her lip. "Shut the fuck up!" Kanika said.

Sheila and Denise moved out of the way and stood by.

"Untie this bitch," Kanika said, and Denise did so.

"Now, tell me everything."

Nikki spit wads of blood into her hand. "I didn't shoot nobody!"

"Bitch, I didn't ask you that!" Specks of spit flew out of Kanika's mouth. "You followed my husband and you helped to kidnap my son. Get the fuck up!"

Nikki stood up slowly and rocked back and forth.

"I don't know who the fuck you are or where the hell you came from, but you fucked with the wrong ones—"

"Look, I didn't know anything about kidnapping—"

Kanika drove a right hook into Nikki, who grabbed Kanika by her hair when she fell. That caused all three women to pounce on Nikki, kicking and beating her until her clothes ripped. Kanika hammered Nikki's face with her fist so many times that Kanika's hand swelled up. Nikki's face was red and blotchy, with her eyes black and blue.

Sheila finally managed to pull Kanika off Nikki. Sheila dragged Kanika down the steps and into her car. Sheila drove Kanika all the way home, with Kanika cursing Nikki every mile of the way.

———

W*hat happened* to your hand?" Tyrell asked when he saw Kanika walk in. It was as big as a basketball.

"I had to beat a bitch's ass," she said in a dry tone. Her body felt tired and exhausted. She lay down on the bed.

"Who?" Tyrell asked, bringing a bag of ice into the room.

"The bitch who was in the elevator with you that day. She's the one who helped Tiffany." Kanika curled up on the bed as Tyrell tended to her hand.

"Sheila and Denise was there?"

Kanika nodded. "Tyrell, I really could've killed that girl. She may be dead. She was just laid out. And you know what? I really don't care if she is dead."

"Yo, that don't matter right now. She ain't dead. So forget that. But I don't wanna hear about you fighting nobody. This ain't a fight for you to finish. It's for me."

Kanika zoned him out as she winced at the pain. "I don't know if I can live like this forever. I am worn down with all this. I want my peace back. I miss Upstate."

"You do?" Tyrell gave her a sarcastic smile. "You know you can always stay there—"

"No, I wanna be with you. I don't know what I'd do if something happened to you while I was living in la-la land. We rise and we fall together. No matter what."

Tyrell kissed her wounded hand. "I wish I could give you a different life—"

"I have everything a woman could want—I have money, a good home, a healthy child, a husband who loves me to death. You've done everything for me, Tyrell. You're all I have."

Tyrell rubbed Kanika's shoulders and kissed them. "The money is good right now, Kanika, and when the money is good, the work gets harder to keep it. I had some niggas blast Rasheeda and Tiffany's crib the other day. They dead."

Kanika's head felt like it was about to explode. "I can't believe this. Did they get anyone?"

"I heard they shot Rasheeda, but not Tiffany."

"The only person who can get Tiffany is me. And I will one day," Kanika said.

On **Thursday** morning, Kanika and Tyrell drove Upstate to visit Ms. Smith. Kanika didn't have her number, but prayed the old woman would be there. They didn't have any other alternative, she thought. Their son's life was at risk. She thought that maybe her mother, from her grave, had put Ms. Smith in her life for a reason. She was ready to see what that reason was.

"You know, I never really appreciated living up here until I left," Kanika said as they rode up the winding tree-lined streets dotted with colonial-style homes. "It's so safe up here."

"That's why I chose it. I'd never sell our house, though. We would always have this place to go to. One day, we'll be just like that old man and woman on the porch." Tyrell pointed to an elderly white couple on their porch, one reading and one sipping a glass of juice.

Kanika smiled as he drove by their quaint home. "Yeah, but we would need a house three times bigger than that."

"We already have one," Tyrell said. He drove up their block, which in the thick of summer was noticeably different from the winter days, with bright greenery everywhere and children riding their bikes.

"She's right here," Kanika said to Tyrell. He slowed his car down. "Let me go in first. I don't want to bombard her all at once."

While Tyrell parked with Little T asleep in the backseat, Kanika took a deep breath. She opened the car door and walked up the steps to Ms. Smith's home. She rang the bell.

It took some time, but Ms. Smith appeared at the door just like it was the first time. Her eyes lit up at the sight of Kanika.

"Honey!" Ms. Smith opened her arms. "Where have you been?"

Kanika walked inside and Ms. Smith guided her to the living room. "So good to see you again."

"Thank you, Ms. Smith." Kanika smiled. "Last time I was here, it was like ten below zero. It's been a while."

Ms. Smith looked at Kanika warmly. "How are you?"

"I'm fine. My family and I just moved to the city for a while. But I need your help." Kanika clasped her hands together.

Ms. Smith extended her hand to Kanika's. "Anything, sweetie."

"My husband and I have ran into some trouble. I need to know if you wouldn't mind watching Little T for us. We'd like him to stay with you."

Ms. Smith brought her hand to her chest. "Well, I—"

"We'll pay you. Money is not a problem," Kanika urged, pulling her checkbook from the tote bag.

"No, please." Ms. Smith smiled uncomfortably. "I'd be honored to watch your son."

Kanika sighed loudly. "Thank you, Ms. Smith, thank you. Anything you need, you just tell us."

Ms. Smith's expression turned serious. "I need to know everything. I need to know what's really going on before I can fully commit."

"My husband and son are outside. Can they come in?" Kanika asked, tinkering with her gold bangles.

"Yes, oh yes," Ms. Smith said, and got up. "Just let them in while I bring us a few drinks."

Kanika waved to Tyrell through the window to come on in.

Within minutes, they were all seated in Ms. Smith's living room. She brought in a pitcher of orange juice with a few glasses. Little T was still asleep in Tyrell's arms.

"My, you two make such a lovely couple," Ms. Smith said as she gently patted Little T's head. "Your baby is absolutely angelic."

Tyrell smiled proudly. "Thank you, and I appreciate how you extended yourself to us. We may not be the model family, but—"

Ms. Smith winked at Kanika. "Your wife did tell me a few things, but, hey, my husband was in the life, too. So I know the ups and downs. But why are you two willing to let me take care of him?"

"I'm just gonna be straight up," Tyrell said, giving Kanika a look that showed it was okay. "They tried to kidnap my son. But they couldn't and killed the nanny instead."

Kanika looked up at the ceiling. She was certain that Ms. Smith was going to change her mind now.

"I see," Ms. Smith said, and sipped on her drink. "You know, about a month or so ago, a young lady came up here looking for you two."

"She did?" Kanika said, leaning forward. "Was she short, with big hips, and looked real ghetto?"

Ms. Smith made a little laugh. "Sort of. She was with some other man in a car. I think the child went to practically every house before she knocked on yours."

"I can't believe she knocked on our door." Kanika moved her hands in the air. "What the hell did she plan to do?"

"She didn't seem like she wanted to see you, but just to know about you. I told her I hadn't seen you, and she seemed furious."

Tyrell touched his goatee. "Yup, she was probably scouting the area. Mike told her where I was at, they couldn't find us, and they went to Brooklyn."

Kanika shook her head. "So, as you can see, Ms. Smith, we just need someone trustworthy who can take care of Little T. He is a good baby. Quiet child."

Ms. Smith opened her arms to take Little T, who had just awakened. He looked up in her face and reached for her glasses. "He's playful," Ms. Smith said, and cooed at him.

Little T laughed as he moved his hands and arms around.

Tyrell put his arms around Kanika when her shoulders fell. She tried her best to hold in her tears. "See, Ms. Smith, he's really no trouble. And I promise, we'll see him all the time. We won't be gone for long."

Ms. Smith put Little T so he could lay his head on her shoulder as she rubbed his back. Kanika noticed how her chest expanded and her eyes peacefully rested on the baby. She knew this moment was special for Ms. Smith, who didn't have her own kids. She looked at Kanika and Tyrell pitifully. "You two have enough to worry about. Little T is in good hands. You just say the word, when you feel it's safe for him again."

"We'll get you everything you need," Tyrell said. "As a matter of fact, Kanika and I will go to the mall today."

"Whatever you think is fine. Come let me show you where he'd be."

Kanika and Tyrell followed Ms. Smith, who still held the baby, upstairs. Her home was a four-story Victorian with dark wood and oak details. They entered a bright-lit room painted in yellow with a sage-colored daybed and several bookcases. "This used to be my husband's reading room. When he passed, years ago, I turned this into a guest room. But there haven't been many guests lately, until now."

Kanika and Tyrell nodded with approval. "The room is perfect. It's sunny, it's quiet," Kanika said, thinking it reminded her of Little T's room down the block.

"You can fit a crib here and a playpen over there. I'd have someone paint it blue, of course," Ms. Smith said. "He'll need some toys."

Kanika laughed. "We'll be back in a few hours. Thank you so much. We'll make this up to you."

Ms. Smith rocked Little T in her arms. "Don't worry, honey, I need all the blessings I can get. You'll understand."

Kanika and Tyrell held each other. "We do."

Several hours later, Kanika and Tyrell returned with bags and boxes of baby food, clothes, and toys. They had also bought a crib that Tyrell assembled right away. It wasn't until 3 A.M. that they left Ms. Smith's home, feeling for the first time since they married that they had done the right thing.

Chapter 16

Tiffany knocked on Lexus's door at an apartment complex about thirty minutes outside of Virginia Beach. It was almost midnight. Though they spoke like nothing had happened, after everything went down with Rasheeda, Tiffany needed to clear the air.

"It's me," Tiffany said, as she pulled her baseball cap low and put on her shades even in the dark. She didn't want to run the risk of anyone recognizing her.

Lexus opened the door. "Everything cool?" he asked. "I thought you was going out of town with Rasheeda this weekend."

Tiffany walked inside, not even caring if he had company. Thankfully, he didn't.

"Niggas is working hard out there," he said as she sat beside him on the couch. "Franky called, told me they practically got a line on Lane Street. Five-oh just turn a blind eye."

Tiffany nodded. "That's not really what I came here for. I know business is good," she said, blowing down on her manicured French nails. "But you and I have some unfinished business."

"True dat," Lexus said. He sat back on the couch. "You start."

"Has Rasheeda asked you about what happened between us?"

Lexus looked at Tiffany funny. "She saw what happened between us. I was blowing that pussy out."

"I mean she didn't ask what's up between us?"

"No," he said, sitting closer to her. "I should be asking what's up between you two."

"Nothing," Tiffany said defensively. "You know how jealous some chicks can be."

"You know, come to think of it, of all the time I known Rasheeda, I never seen her with a nigga. She either solo or with some bitch."

Tiffany looked over Lexus's shoulder at a collection of DVD movies, all gangsta and karate flicks.

"You fucked her?" Lexus asked in a matter-of-fact tone.

"Maybe I did—what that got to do with you?"

Lexus's face relaxed. "I figured that much. It don't make me no difference. I still wanna get with you. We can do big things together. Real big things."

Tiffany walked her fingers along his leg up to between his thighs. Even through the thick denim, she still felt it.

"This real big thing?" She unzipped his jeans.

Lexus's mouth stretched into a grin as he helped her take out his size.

She caressed his hot silky brown skin. "You know, I did forget to do something the last time."

"I didn't give you a chance," he said, grazing his dick across her lips.

Tiffany opened her mouth and sucked gently on the head of his dick, licking the sides up and down.

Lexus guided her head around his dick as she ran her tongue along his balls and back up again. She slipped him inside her mouth until he couldn't go any farther. Lexus moaned in plea-sure as Tiffany gave him the ultimate spit shine.

When she was done, Lexus was the only one out of breath.

Tiffany wiped the corners of her mouth. "So you were saying?"

Lexus zipped his pants back up. "I was saying we need to help each other. I need a bitch like you with me. What you think?"

Tiffany liked the look in Lexus's eyes. He seemed sincere, but he wasn't Saliq. Saliq could own her body and her mind with just a whisper in her ear. "I don't know," Tiffany said. "I can barely talk about a man around Rasheeda without her catching a fit. It's too much drama. My money comes first."

"A'ight," Lexus said. He gazed through Tiffany's white blouse at her hardened nipples. "But you can't be with Rasheeda forever. You need a man. We can have our own shit."

"Not interested, sorry," Tiffany said as she rose to leave—but the more she thought about it, the better it sounded.

The next morning, Tiffany joined Rasheeda for breakfast. Her friend was preparing waffles and bacon, after having fired the cook and maid the week before. Tiffany had figured Rasheeda was getting more paranoid by the week, with everything that was going down. She didn't trust anyone.

"Whatsup," Rasheeda said, breaking the silence at the table. "My food ain't good enough?" she asked with a sarcastic smile.

"The food is good—I'm just tired."

Rasheeda sipped the champagne from one of her crystal flutes. "Where was you last night?"

"I was out, trying to relax," Tiffany said. She spread some but-ter on the light, tasty waffles. She took a bite. "These are good."

"You was with Lexus, right?"

Tiffany took another small bite. "We was together for a minute. What time you got in?"

"Before you."

They both ate in silence for a few minutes.

"You know, I been thinking," Tiffany began. "And I really didn't wanna get you caught up in all my family drama. You got shot. Your house got riddled with bullets, and I'm all in one piece. It's not fair for me to keep living here."

"So what you saying?" Rasheeda asked. She motioned her fork in the air. "You wanna leave?"

"Maybe I should get my own house. I have more than enough money. I got too much money I don't do shit with."

Rasheeda poured herself some more champagne. "So, now you wanna fuckin' bounce after you get what you need."

"That's not it," Tiffany said, trying to remain cool, though Rasheeda was hot. "I need my space."

"So, that's it? This has nothing to do with Lexus?"

"Right," Tiffany lied.

"So let me get this straight: You wanna go spend half a million dollars on a house all by yourself, so you can have space and give up living in a three-million-dollar house where you can have more space and none of the bills. Did I get that right?"

Tiffany closed her eyes for a moment. "I guess. I don't know."

"You know," Rasheeda said, rising from the table. "Go ahead. Get your own place. Do what you want. I have no problem with it."

Tiffany looked at Rasheeda, shocked at her sudden change in attitude. "Are you sure?"

"Yeah, look, whatever. I may not like it, but you your own woman." Rasheeda took her glass of champagne from the table and said, "Do you."

O*n Tuesday* night, Rasheeda had her top escorts at her house. Tonight was a big one, because one of the major players in the rap game was gonna be in town. He was throwing an after party following his show and needed several of her chicks for him and his boys.

"Okay, now, I need all of you bitches at the hotel before they get there. Do not even think of getting to the hotel a minute after three A.M. You will need to make your own way there, but a car will take you back home—"

"Shit, I ain't trying to go home," said Sapphire, a medium-brown-skinned older girl in the group who had a silky black weave. "Not if I get lucky. I'm trying to go back to New York with that nigga."

"I don't do business with sluts," Rasheeda said as she puffed on her cigarette. "Remember, you bitches are not groupies. You are above that status. You are all hoes, a whole different ball game. You get something in return." Everyone nodded and cheered in agreement. "Tell the niggas you need them to sign the receipts," Rasheeda said as they trailed out the door to the car in their highest heels, spandex bodysuits, fishnet stockings, and miniskirts.

Tiffany sat by and listened, as usual. It amused her how Rasheeda ran her escort business like a well-oiled machine. It was strictly business to her, except when it came to Diana.

Diana wasn't going out tonight. Rasheeda had arranged for them to chill together, to Tiffany's dismay.

Rasheeda had been ignoring Tiffany for the last several days. At first it didn't bother her, because she did need the space. But after the third day, Tiffany was getting nervous. She didn't realize how much she counted on Rasheeda. She needed her.

Tiffany fixed herself a sandwich in the kitchen while she tried to block out the laughter coming from the den, where Rasheeda and Diana were drinking and watching a movie.

Tiffany stood at the door, wanting to join them, but Rasheeda didn't even look at her. She took her food upstairs to the bedroom. It ran through her mind to call Lexus. She thought maybe they could go out together. But he was supposed to be working as her second in charge, not as her man. She wasn't ready to cross that line yet. Strictly sex, she thought, was good enough. She pushed down her desire for more.

A few hours passed, and Tiffany noticed that the house was silent. It was 2 A.M., and she walked downstairs to the kitchen for something to drink.

She noticed Diana asleep on the couch, her panties by her feet.

Tiffany tapped her shoulder. "Where's Rasheeda?"

Diana half opened her eyes. "Oh!" Diana giggled. "She had to make a quick run somewhere."

"So what you still doing here?" Tiffany flicked on the lights.

Diana sat up and blocked the light from her eyes with her hands. "What the fuck is your problem?"

Tiffany threw Diana's clothes at her. "Get the fuck out, bitch."

Diana flew off the couch and pushed Tiffany. Tiffany whaled on Diana, knocking her in the face several times. She lost complete control as she beat Diana down. The anger seemed to come out of nowhere, she thought. She pounced on Diana with her fists until they hurt.

"What now, ho? What!" Tiffany said, hopping around Diana like a champion fighter. "I been wanting to kick your ass since I saw you."

Diana limped around, holding her bloody mouth. "Oh my God, wait till I tell Rasheeda. You are so over, bitch."

"Rasheeda would never choose you over me!" Tiffany said,

feeling a greater surge of adrenaline. "You can't take Rasheeda from me."

Diana leaped at Tiffany again, but this time Tiffany grabbed the lamp on the table and knocked Diana across her head with it. Diana flipped over the couch and landed on her back. Tiffany jumped on Diana's motionless body and choked her until Diana's eyes fell back into her head.

"Bitch!" Tiffany yelled repeatedly at Diana. She saw everyone she hated in Diana's pretty face.

Tiffany let Diana go and backed up. "Get up!" But she noticed that Diana didn't move. "Ho, get your bitch ass up!" Tiffany bent down and listened for Diana's heart. She heard nothing.

Goose bumps covered Tiffany's body. Her chest deflated when she realized what she had done. Diana was dead. There she was, she thought, taking another person's life for no good reason. She convinced herself that she was just bad all around. *I stopped giving a fuck a while ago.*

She dialed Lexus. "Get over here, now!" she said, and hung up. She quickly wiped tears from her eyes.

She listened for Diana's heart several times, hoping she would come back somehow. She prayed that Rasheeda wouldn't walk through that door. Tiffany cleaned up the blood around her and burned Diana's clothes down on the backyard grill. She did everything in a daze.

Finally, Lexus arrived with his gun pulled. The first thing he saw was Diana's body. He looked down at it but didn't say a word.

"Do something!" Tiffany said. "I need to get rid of this!"

Lexus turned to Tiffany with a confused look. "What the fuck happened? Ain't this Rasheeda chick?"

"The bitch attacked me. That's what happened," Tiffany said, breathing hard and quick.

"And you killed her?"

"I didn't mean to—we were fighting and I just lost it. She made me do it," Tiffany said frantically..

"You did this because you were jealous—" Lexus put on a mischievous smile. "—right?"

"Do what I ordered you to do," Tiffany said in a cold tone.

"Fine, but Rasheeda—"

"Rasheeda, nothing. She can never know this."

Lexus grabbed Diana up and took her body to the trunk of his car. Tiffany watched him speed off into the night.

Chapter 17

A **few weeks later**, at the end of July, Kanika noticed a change in Tyrell. It had been a little over a month since their son began his stay with Ms. Smith. Tyrell had been spending less time at home, and when he was home, he was asleep or to himself. She had let it slide, but was beginning to wonder.

"Hey, baby," Kanika said when Tyrell climbed into bed with her in the evening. She rubbed his back and nibbled on his shoulders.

Tyrell's back stiffened. He didn't even make a move for more.

"You okay?" Kanika asked. She touched her nose with his. It had been almost a week since they made love. They hadn't gone that long since they broke up over a year ago. She needed to feel Tyrell all over her.

Tyrell grunted something and turned his face away like he wanted to sleep.

Kanika felt absolutely rejected, but she wasn't giving up. She climbed on top of him and pressed her pussy on his back. "I want some," she purred.

Tyrell didn't budge, and Kanika slid off. "Talk to me, Tyrell. What the hell is going on?"

He finally turned over on his back and covered his eyes with arms. "I'm tired."

"So am I, and I can't understand it. I had more energy when Little T was around."

"That ain't what I mean," Tyrell said.

Kanika lowered her body next to him. "What is it?"

"Money is tight. The Colombians raised the cost on me, and I can't afford to keep up with the demand. Big Gee says we only have enough product for a couple weeks."

Kanika winced. She couldn't believe money was an issue. Everything seemed like normal. "You gotta buy more, Tyrell."

"Yo, I just told you, shit is tight. I gotta get a new connect. Muthafuckas could be trying to drive me out. Times are changing. It ain't like when Tony was coming up. There's new laws, new product, heroin is coming back, crack is going out. Shit is getting complicated."

Kanika racked her brain for what to say. Times were changing. Tyrell was one of the last of his breed. Everyone else was either in jail or dead. Kanika felt they were fighting for their lives. "We'll come up with something."

"I need some sleep," Tyrell said, rolling over.

Kanika flicked on the lights. "Hell no. We gotta work this out now. We gotta find money—"

"I got an idea," Tyrell said.

Kanika listened.

"We can sell the Upstate house. It's worth almost a million dollars."

"And live where?" Kanika said, hating the idea.

"We'd stay here until we can find someplace else. Just as nice. Because when I push out the rest on the streets, I'll have paper for the rest of the year. Then I'll have the same problem again."

"Ain't no other ways?"

"Unless I go to Colombia and negotiate with those mutha-fuckas. I can bring Big Gee with me."

Kanika didn't like that idea either. She had remembered the few times Tony used to go, before Tyrell came on the scene. Tony dreaded it because he called it "cottoning." He felt he had to bow down, and the Colombians had a way of making him feel like shit. But everything always ended up better when he came back. "You do what you gotta do, even if it means selling the house."

Several days later, boxes arrived at their Manhattan apart-ment. Tyrell had put the house up for sale.

Kanika wasn't sure why, but this made her furious. She thought he wouldn't go there, but he did. It seemed selfish, she thought. It was their first home. She had expected them to talk it through some more. Maybe even see how things went in Co-lombia. But he up and sold it. She felt like they had no place to run to.

"Tyrell, we need to talk," Kanika said as he helped some of the movers bring the boxes in.

"Not now," Tyrell said, ignoring her. He walked back out.

Kanika waited until he had a moment. Then she approached him again when the movers left.

"Why couldn't you wait till you got back from Colombia?"

He gave her the once-over.

Kanika took a few deep breaths. She reminded herself that he was under stress. But a part of her was like, *fuck it*.

"Where are we gonna go to now? You could've waited."

"Look, I do what I think is right. I would never put us in any trouble. I felt it was right to do it now," he said, glaring at her.

"So where we gonna go when shit gets rough again? Niggas still know where we live."

"Yo, let me worry about that."

"No, drop that Mr. Man shit right now. You and I work together. You can't make all the decisions on your own."

"You better watch your mouth," Tyrell said as he opened a can of beer. "You know, lately you really been trying me."

Kanika walked up to him. "Fuck you! You ain't the only one around here stressin'. You ain't the only one with problems. I need attention, I need to feel like I'm included. This is my life, too."

Tyrell walked past her, and Kanika grabbed his arm.

He shoved her against the door. "Don't ever fucking touch me. Understand?" he said, clenching his teeth. He held her chin in his hand.

Kanika rubbed her jaw when he let it go. "You put your hands on me again—"

He pushed her. "Now what?"

Kanika slapped him across the face and left the imprint of her wedding ring on his cheek.

Tyrell grabbed her by her arms, lifted her up, and body-slammed her on the couch. Kanika kicked him in his chest as he grabbed her legs and dragged her to the floor. They tousled around the ground, Kanika scratching him in the face several times, until he held her down.

"So you wanna fight me like a man now? I'll beat your ass just like Tony did your mama. Is that what you want?"

Kanika didn't move. She couldn't believe what was happening. Tyrell's face was scratched up with red lines of blood. "Go ahead, hit me. Do it!"

Tyrell wanted every fiber of his being to slap Kanika hard enough to knock her into next week, but he couldn't bring himself to do it. He let her go.

"You wanna be like your mama so bad, you would want to get fucked up like she did."

"You told me you'd beat my ass."

"I was talking shit!" Tyrell said, shaking his head. "Yo, I ain't got time for this shit. If you wanna fight like your mama and Tony did, I ain't with it. That ain't me. *This* ain't me," he said, then grabbed his car keys and jetted out the door.

Kanika was alone the following day. Tyrell and Big Gee had taken a private jet to Colombia. She missed him already. She was embarrassed by how she'd acted the other day. She couldn't even explain to herself where the anger came from. Maybe she had been through too much during the past year, she thought. She wanted to make it up to him when he came back. It had been only a few months since they got married, and she wanted the honeymoon feeling to last. She wanted to be the perfect wife, not the little girl who was so in love with him. She needed to be the woman she knew her mother would be proud of.

After leaving the spa around 6 P.M., Kanika drove to the nearest Victoria's Secret, armed and ready with her American Express card. As soon as she entered the store, she swore the salesperson smelled it. "Can I help you with something?" asked the young black girl dressed in all black. She was light-skinned with a ponytail and glossy lips. Kanika had thought they looked about the same age.

"Actually, yeah," Kanika said, not sure where to start. "I need a little bit of everything."

"I'll be happy to help you. We got these panties right here on sale—"

"Just show me the hot shit. I don't care about sales," Kanika said, walking down the lingerie aisle.

The salesgirl pulled out a few outfits for her—a black sheer teddie, a two-piece red bra-and-panty set, and a icy blue up-front nightie. Kanika tried on the clothes and wasn't too impressed.

She handed the salesperson the items. "I need something a little naughty," Kanika said. Her eyes caught a purple-and-black satin garter set. "This is nice."

"I was just about to show you that," said the salesgirl. She handed Kanika an outfit in her size. "I'll pick up a few other things while you try that on."

About an hour later, Kanika had tried on half the lingerie items. She settled on a few sexy pieces, some panties, scented creams, and lacy bras. She definitely had stepped up her game. She wanted to look edible the next time Tyrell saw her.

"Thank you," Kanika said. She was gathering selections to take to the register.

"I'm sorry," the salesgirl said, and gave Kanika a strange look. "You seem so familiar. Did you used to live on Halsey Street?"

Kanika tilted her head to the side and peeped the girl's name tag, which read LIA.

"I did. But I'm not sure we know each other."

"Yeah," the girl said, raising her finger. "Your mom was Waleema, right?"

"Yes." Kanika nodded. She smiled. It was good to hear her mother's name.

"Wow, I am so sorry about what happened to her. The block has never been the same, girl."

"Well, things happen. She's in a better place," Kanika said, her voice a little shaky.

"Are you still with Tyrell?"

That's when Kanika's expression changed. "We're married," Kanika said. It wasn't a big deal, because everyone knew she and Tyrell were a couple.

"Damn, girl, that ring is hot," the salesgirl said, taking Kanika's hand. "He was the fine brother who used to run with Tony. I hear he is making moves again. What is it like being married to him?"

Kanika didn't say anything else when she caught on to the salesgirl. It was like Lia wanted to know more. "Excuse me, I really gotta go."

When Kanika left, she passed by the salesgirl again and didn't look in her direction. But she felt the woman's eyes glued to her back.

Chapter 18

This is crazy," **Rasheeda** huffed as she slammed down the phone. "Two weeks and no Diana. You said she just bounced that night for no reason?"

Tiffany layed down on the couch in the living room after feeling sick for a few days. For two weeks, Tiffany watched as Rasheeda tried to track Diana down. "Yeah, she sounded like something happened."

Rasheeda looked down on her desk. She shook her head. "What I hate about what I do is that I can never call the muthafuckin' cops. Man," she sighed. "She was my top bitch. She and I go way back to even before I got in the game—"

Tiffany yawned. "You sound like you was in love or something."

"Not in love, but I had love for her. How could she do me like this? Just split and shit?" Rasheeda asked. "You were home that night when she left, right?"

"Yes, I was. I was in the kitchen, she got all bouncy when she got some phone call and left."

Rasheeda continued staring at Tiffany.

Tiffany put her hands in the air. "That's all I remember. I didn't know I was supposed to be a fuckin' babysitter."

Rasheeda's chest swelled. "You know, I have a funny feeling you two got into some shit that night—"

Tiffany's heartbeat accelerated.

"Whatever happened between you and Diana, I'll find out about that shit. Nothing ever slips by me. Understand?"

Tiffany stayed quiet.

"And look at you. You look all tired and sick. You know, I'm really beginning to wonder how useful you are. Get your ass off my couch."

Tiffany stumbled off the couch.

"What is wrong with you?"

"Rasheeda, I am just tired and stressed. That's all. I need to see a doctor. I haven't been feeling good at all," Tiffany said, appealing to Rasheeda's sympathy.

Rasheeda's eyes turned to concern. She brought her hand to Tiffany's forehead. "I'm taking you to my doctor. She'll give you whatever you need."

Tiffany wondered if her plan had just backfired.

Rasheeda took Tiffany to Dr. Slatkin, one of the premier doctors in the Virginia Beach area. Tiffany didn't have a doctor of her own.

Tiffany and Rasheeda waited patiently in the reception area. She didn't have to try too hard to play sick, because she really thought she was coming down with something. She thought the sooner she got the visit over with, the better.

Dr. Slatkin called Tiffany into the room, where she did a complete examination and took a urine sample.

Dr. Slatkin left Tiffany alone in the room. A few minutes later, Rasheeda came in.

"Need some company?" Rasheeda asked, and closed the door behind her.

Tiffany gave her a weak smile.

"Listen, I just want to apologize for being so hard on you lately. I just wanna see you do good in this game. I've seen a lot of people get distracted and fuck up. I'll always have your back as long as you have mine. Remember that." Rasheeda softly touched Tiffany's face.

Tiffany closed her eyes at Rasheeda's touch. "I'll always have your back. And I'm sorry about Diana. You know how some women are. Real flaky, but I'll never be like that."

Dr. Slatkin knocked and came back in the room with the test results. "Okay, ladies. The urine results show that your HCG levels in the urine are really high. It means you're pregnant."

Tiffany felt happily excited; then in the next moment, her shoulders collapsed.

"Pregnant?" Rasheeda asked, looking at Tiffany. "By Lexus?"

Dr. Slatkin stood by uncomfortably.

"Yes!" Tiffany said. "He was the only one. I don't know what the hell I'm gonna do." Tears welled up in her eyes.

"Oh, I know." Rasheeda folded her arms across her chest. "And you do, too."

"We have several options here," Dr. Slatkin began. "But you should think about it before you decide."

"Yeah, I will." Tiffany hopped off the patient bed, and she and Rasheeda left.

When they were alone in the car, Rasheeda said, "You're getting an abortion."

Tiffany shuddered at the words. She thought there was a life inside her that could give her the love she had been looking for. But she convinced herself that she had to do the right thing. "I have to tell Lexus."

"You ain't got to say shit to him!"

"I do! This ain't simple. I'm pregnant. I don't want this baby, but it may just be working out like I wanted."

Rasheeda and Tiffany's eyes locked.

"Are you thinking what I'm thinking?" Rasheeda asked as she hit the gas.

Tiffany drove up to Lexus's apartment late that night. She was going to tell him what she had decided. A small, quiet part of her wished she could be happy about it. But the only man she ever wanted a baby by was Saliq. She couldn't take the chance of having a baby with Lexus and having him get killed, too, like Saliq. Life in the game could end any day, she thought, and when it did, she didn't want to be the one left holding the bag.

They lay in bed, their sweaty bodies entangled with each other. Tiffany couldn't get enough of his built, healthy physique.

She climbed on top, rubbing her pussy onto his dick. "What if I got pregnant one of these times?"

Lexus ran his hands over her big ass. "I know you wouldn't keep it."

"Should I?"

"I mean, if you want—"

"I could not see myself with no kid. I still got too much money to get," Tiffany said, pointing her finger in his face.

"Is you trying to tell me something?"

"Do you love me?"

Lexus squirmed underneath her. "I could love you if we spend more time together."

Tiffany laughed. "I have enough love for myself. You couldn't handle this, anyway."

"Maybe not," he said, sliding her off him.

"I'm pregnant," she revealed with her back turned to him.

A quietness stayed in the air for about ten minutes.

"It's mine?" Lexus asked.

"Yes."

"Well, I already said—"

"Listen, nigga." Tiffany rolled over in his face. "I don't need you to tell me what you want or think. I'm telling you simply because you might see me with a big-ass bump soon walking around here—"

"I was about to say that I'll help you take care of it." Lexus sat up slowly in the bed.

"Don't flatter yourself," Tiffany said. "I ain't even sure I'm gonna keep it full term."

"But it's my child, too—"

"Nigga, shut the fuck up! This ain't about you. It's about me. You know the baby is yours, but not everyone does—"

"So, what that mean?"

Tiffany hopped out of the bed and pinned her naked body against Lexus. "It may be Tyrell's—"

Lexus's eyes grew small. "You trying to tell that nigga the baby is his? How?"

"Oh, I got this little plan. I'm gonna keep this baby as long as I can. Maybe I'll give birth to it, maybe I won't."

"That's my child, too. I don't know how I feel about you giving some nigga the claim to my kid." Lexus looked disgusted.

"It's my body, my baby. I didn't want to get pregnant. And since when are you the model father?"

Lexus's face relaxed. "Whatever, I still think it's wack what you doin'. There's other ways, and it ain't using an unborn baby."

"I don't care what you say. I have all the answers to what I need to do up inside me," Tiffany said, patting her stomach.

Chapter 19

It had been a few days since Tyrell got back from Colombia. He negotiated a deal where he'd get more territory, more volume, but not a bigger cut on the money. He was now able to meet the demand to cover Brooklyn, Queens, and parts of the Bronx, but the cash flow was the same. That wasn't enough for him. He needed more. He wanted to make *more* than Tony ever had, not as much as he had.

"Do you want to come?" Kanika asked Tyrell as he brushed his teeth. She was getting set to see Little T Upstate.

"Nah, I gotta make a couple of runs." He rinsed his mouth out. "I'll be back tonight."

"Little T misses you, I'm sure. You can't take a few hours?"

"No," he said, splashing water on his face. "I'll see him next time. Make sure you give him a big hug from Pops."

"Yeah, I will," Kanika said as she checked the mail on the dining room table. There was a letter from their credit card company threatening to close their account for nonpayment. Kanika read the letter three times before she understood what was going down. She opened another letter from the mortgage company. They were starting foreclosure proceedings. Kanika almost fell out.

"Did you see these?" Kanika waved the letters in the air. "We paid these!"

Tyrell patted his face dry as he looked at her. "Not lately," he grumbled, and turned the shower on.

"What!" Kanika said. She flung the letters at him. "You haven't paid our bills? That's why you wanted to sell the house, because you stopped paying for it!"

Tyrell looked up at the ceiling in frustration. "Didn't I tell you we was having some money problems?"

"Not like this."

"Well, I got a lot of shit on my mind. The money I got from my connects ain't change much. Times are tight. Just deal with it."

Kanika put her hands on her hips. "What else don't I know, Tyrell? Are they gonna kick us out this apartment, too? Are we losing everything?"

"Excuse me, I need to take a shower," Tyrell said as he stepped in and pulled the curtain closed.

Kanika pulled it back open. "We need money. The barbershop and the spa are not cutting it."

"It's always about money with you," he said, while water ran against his back. "You ain't got no concept of the fucking stress I'm under. I ain't used to this shit either. You further complicating it with your demands. Fuck that!"

"Fuck *you*!" said Kanika before she stormed out of the bathroom and left the apartment. She felt like a complete idiot for buying all that lingerie the other day.

After several hours, Kanika finally made it to Ms. Smith's home. She had her own key. As soon as she walked in, the sweet smells of vanilla and apples surrounded her. The house glowed in soft yellows with fresh flowers and plants in the foyer.

"Ms. Smith?" Kanika called as she walked farther inside. She peeked in the living room, but no one was there.

She crept up the steps and saw Ms. Smith in the little room Little T was staying in. She was reading him a story. Kanika leaned against the door. Her son was bonding with another woman. Little T's eyes followed every movement of Ms. Smith's lips. He looked calm, peaceful, like he didn't even know his mommy had been gone. Kanika thought maybe he had even forgotten.

"That was beautiful, Ms. Smith," Kanika said after the old woman closed the book. "My mother used to read to me many times."

Ms. Smith handed Little T over to Kanika and smiled. "Have you ever read to your son?"

"No," Kanika said. "I just thought he was too young. But now I see how he can really sit and listen at just a few months old. It even looked like he understood."

"Children are very smart," Ms. Smith said, bringing a bottle to Little T's lips. "Never underestimate them."

Little T fussed with the bottle and began to cry.

"That's right—he may not be hungry now. He usually eats about three P.M.," Kanika said. She took the bottle from him. She wiped his mouth, but he kept wiggling around in distress.

"Let me see," Ms. Smith said, and took the baby back.

Kanika watched in awe as Little T suckled the bottle like it was his last. He was calm again. That was like a blade stuck in her chest. It had been only a month, she thought.

"I can't stand this," Kanika spit out. "I hate being away from my son."

Ms. Smith rubbed Kanika's back as she fed Little T. "It's your choice, baby. You don't have to be away from him. You can even stay with us if you like."

Kanika wiped a tear from her eye. "I can't leave Tyrell right now. He's really going through some stress—"

Ms. Smith turned Little T over on her shoulder to burp him. "What about you, my dear? When does your life begin?"

"He and my son are my life. They are my family. I just wish he had a different job, that's all," Kanika said, managing a smile.

Little T had dozed off on Ms. Smith's shoulder, and she placed him in the crib. Kanika and Ms. Smith walked downstairs to the kitchen, where there was a Crock-Pot simmering with a stew of chicken, dumplings, and root vegetables. The scent it left in the air gave Kanika a nostalgic feeling of being back in her mother's kitchen.

"Hungry?" Ms. Smith said, stirring the Crock-Pot.

Kanika nodded her head. She and Ms. Smith sat down together for the meal.

"You know, I hope you're not worried about how long Little T has been here with me. It's not like he's gonna forget you. He notices you're not around, especially when he tries to pull on my boobies," Ms. Smith said, and stuck out her thin chest.

Kanika chewed on the dumpling while trying to stop herself from laughing. "I guess, but I just miss him. It's like since he left, Tyrell and I have been at it. He's so focused on the streets that he hasn't paid our bills on time. Also because he's not making the money he used to make. Little T gave us both purpose, he calmed us down, now we're at each other's throats because we have nothing to distract us—"

"Well, honey," Ms. Smith said, patting her mouth with a napkin. "You're dealing with the real relationship when it's just the two of you, no buffers, no barriers. This is how you two really are."

Kanika ate her soup and wondered for a moment. "I know he loves me. I love him to death."

"That's not enough sometimes. But you two will get through this. I'm sure you've been through worse."

"We have."

"Just understand he will never leave that life. It'll always be his mistress."

Kanika returned from Upstate the next day. She had decided to cool off overnight. She thought that when she got home, Tyrell would have cooled off, too. But he wasn't even there.

Kanika got her mind off things by cleaning. She didn't want to go to the spa and deal with anyone or even have him think that she was tracking him down. Maybe she needed to be alone some more.

As she folded and put away some of Tyrell's clothes in his closet, she could still smell his scent on them. It was clean after-shave smell she'd always remember from the first time she met him. She tucked his socks away in the drawer and noticed something.

There was a small piece of paper with a number scribbled on it. Her stomach turned into knots suddenly. She knew what that was about. She was tempted to call it, but decided to fall back. She tucked it in her jeans pocket and kept on cleaning.

But several hours later, she still couldn't get the number out of her mind. When Tyrell came home around 5 P.M., Kanika decided to find out the story.

While Tyrell was in the bathroom, she went through his cell phone to find a number that matched the one she had. She came up on one. He had called it several times over the last few weeks, and the person had called him a few times today. Kanika quickly dialed the number and heard a female voice.

"Who is this?" Kanika politely asked.

"You called my phone," said the girl on the other end.

Fuck it, Kanika thought. She didn't want to get into any petty squabble. All she needed was the girl's name. "This is Kanika. Who is this?"

She heard the girl's voice break down from confident to feeble. "Oh, hi, this is Lia. Uhm—"

Kanika squeezed the phone in her hand. It was the girl from Victoria's Secret. Her intuition had told her something was off with the salesgirl.

"I guess you found my number."

Kanika clicked off the phone. She didn't want to waste her precious energy on the trick, she thought to herself, when Tyrell was right there.

"Listen," Tyrell said as he buckled his pants in front of her. "I may have to run out again. I got a meeting with some people downtown. Big Gee need me."

"What kind of meeting?" Kanika asked, her temperature rising by the minute.

"You know what kind of meeting. We need to handle business. Get money," he said, searching for his phone. "Where my phone?"

"I don't know." Kanika walked to the bedroom. He followed her.

"Where's my phone?" he repeated more loudly. "I had it on the nightstand."

"Is this the person you wanna to talk to?" Kanika shoved the piece of paper in his face.

"What's your point?" Tyrell said, staring at the number. "I don't know this person."

Kanika pulled out his phone and dialed.

He snatched the phone away from her.

"That number came up many times on your phone. You fucking

somebody named Lia? I didn't even get a chance to see the text messages."

Tyrell sat down on the bed. "Now you going through my shit? Accusing me of fucking somebody? Yo, this shit is wack."

"And I saw the bitch when I went to Victoria's Secret last week. She ain't even your type! At least get a better bitch than me." Kanika flicked her finger in his face. "You are fucking her. What other reason would you need to call a bitch for?"

Tyrell's chest caved in. Kanika was waiting for more of a fight from him, for more resistance. He almost seemed relieved.

"I can't do this," Tyrell said, throwing his hands in the air. "I got you, I got the three businesses, I got bills, I got niggas wanting me dead— You think I got time for this? All this arguing you wanna do—"

Kanika ground her teeth. "So what you saying? Can't do what? Be honest? Be a man?"

Tyrell stood up and faced her. "So, now you wanna judge my manhood? You finally crossed the damn line. I don't need this. This can't work with us anymore."

Kanika swallowed hard. She wasn't expecting that at all. She ran after him as he left the room. She pushed him against the wall. "You leaving me?" Her eyes swelled with fear.

He took her hands off him. "The way we been living lately ain't good for business. I can't do what I want when I got you on my case. I can't make money—"

Kanika grew silent and looked at him intently, with an eerie calm.

"This is it for me," he said, and shook his head.

"You wanna leave me *now*?" The images of her mother and Tony being killed, Tyrell's confession that he'd been involved, them fleeing her father, who'd tried to kill them both, his vow to love her through life and death all ran through her mind. "After all we been through, now you wanna leave?" she asked again.

Tyrell's expression changed, as if he didn't know the impact of what he had just said. But it was too late to take it back.

She bore her eyes into him. "You are *not* leaving me."

Tyrell was at a loss for words.

Chapter 20

In his heart, Tyrell knew he could never leave Kanika. In fact, he couldn't even imagine it. But with the stress they had been under, he really needed some time to think. He had nightmares about Kanika leaving him for not living up to what they had dreamed. He was embarrassed sometimes. Things were definitely harder to come by now than it was when he was coming up. The drug hustle was ever-changing, due to the body count from neighborhood crack wards and tough sentencing that had cats locked up for twenty-five years to life. Sometimes Tyrell wondered if Tony's death was bringing him to his own death. The jewels, the luxury cars, the girls, the hustle never compared to a peaceful night's sleep. He couldn't tell when he'd last had one. Though it had been a moment since he had been with another woman besides Kanika, Lia just happened to be at the right place at the right time. He was tempted to sleep with a young trick from the block. But instead, he took her calls and acted like he was willing. He didn't know how, but Kanika had taken over his mind and soul—and his body, too. He wasn't good for anyone, including his wife, he thought.

"Good afternoon, Ms. Smith. Is Kanika there?" Tyrell said, and waited for her to get the phone.

"Hello?" Kanika said on the other end.

"When you coming home?" It had been about a week since she'd gone Upstate, after their fight.

"Soon. I really think we needed this time apart to clear our heads," she said.

"I agree. How about you come home tonight?"

After a moment of silence, Kanika said, "Not yet. I think it's better if I stay up here a little while longer and bond with Little T."

"Yo, I miss you. And I swear nothing ever happened with Lia—"

"I believe you," Kanika said in a firm tone. "Maybe we just needed a break."

Tyrell nodded his head. "I need my partner back home."

"I hear you," Kanika sighed.

"I'm supposed to be going to this party with Big Gee—one of his rapper cousins is having a birthday party. You sure you can't come?"

"I'm sure."

"I need you home."

"Soon, Tyrell," Kanika said, and hung up.

While she had been gone, he did get several things done. Though money wasn't flowing, it wasn't fleeing either. When he came back from Colombia, he and Big Gee infiltrated the market with five-dollar bags of crack, something newer hustlers were already doing. It helped some. But things could have been better, he thought, if less of his low-ranked corner dealers weren't taking time out to get in the rap game.

*N*eed a drink, man?" Big Gee asked Tyrell, who leaned up against the wall at his cousin Suave's party being held at a three-story house in Jamaica, Queens.

"Yeah, let me get a lil' something," Tyrell said, taking a glass of cognac from Big Gee. They both scanned the dark room, and it was everything that a party was supposed to be—lots of girls, good music, and nonstop alcohol and weed. Big Gee made the acquaintance of several females, who whispered in his ear, but he always kept Tyrell's back. Lord knew anything could happen, at any moment.

Several girls in tight-fitting jeans and skintight bodysuits eyed Tyrell. Some even engaged him in small talk, but he wasn't with it. It seemed like the more cool, laid-back, and reserved he stayed, the more the girls wanted a piece of him. One danced up on him when a reggae song came on, and he backed away. He wasn't about to disrespect his wife again. Kanika knew about half of Queens and all of Brooklyn. It was possible anything could get back to her. Even if he looked at a girl too long, it could be drama.

Around 1 A.M., Suave came on the mic and spit a few rhymes for the crowd. Tyrell thought he was nice, but even after several glasses of Henny, he wasn't that impressed. He walked to a dark room, where there were a few folks drinking and laughing. No one seemed to notice when he kicked back in the chair, finished his last glass, and just chilled. After some time, the room emptied. It was just him. He heard the pounding of music against the walls. He wondered what time it was.

Then a knock came on the door. He wasn't sure if he had turned temporarily blind or what, but he didn't see anything but a curvy silhouette until the low light flicked on.

His head was still woozy from the alcohol, but the girl was familiar. He knew her.

"Tyrell?" The voice purred his name in the dim room. "'Member me?"

Tyrell rubbed his eyes and squinted at her. "Tiffany?"

Tiffany walked up to Tyrell slowly. "You would think the last place we'd be alone is a bedroom, right?" She giggled.

Tyrell closed his eyes and lay back on the chair. "What the hell you doin' here?"

"I was in the neighborhood." Tiffany grinned, her fingers tracing the goatee around Tyrell's mouth.

"You look different," he said, glancing at her ample breasts and juicy thighs, which her denim minidress did little to hide. His head throbbed, and he lay back again.

Tiffany sat carefully on his lap.

Tyrell flexed to push her off, but his body was weak. She felt good. All he needed was some sleep, he thought.

"I think you and I can do big business together. Just think of how much bread we can get if we combined our territories. I'm sure you can use a few of my connects. I know I can use some of yours."

"What?" Tyrell asked, opening his eyes slightly. She sounded like she was rambling, and he couldn't understand.

"Do you know anyone who may be interested in a girl like me? Someone who can help me take over? Not your turf, but help me branch out in my area?"

"No," Tyrell said, rubbing his aching head.

She kissed his nose, then his lips.

"Yo," he said, finally alert to what was happening. "What the fuck? You tryin' to fuck a nigga?"

Tiffany hopped off him, turned over, and lifted up her skirt. "You could have all this ass, Tyrell. No one has to know." She grabbed his hand to touch it.

Tyrell pulled his hand back from her soft, doughy skin. "I'm out," he said, walking quickly to the door.

Tiffany jumped in front of him and grabbed him by the neck.

She planted a deep, long kiss on his lips until they stumbled on the bed.

"Mmm, I love the taste of Henny on a man's lips," she said, licking hers and pulling down his pants as fast as she could. "Let me suck ya dick," she begged.

Tyrell rolled her over and held her down with his hands. "You a crazy bitch. And if you ever come around my family, I'll kill you like I killed your daddy."

Tyrell slowly got off the bed and backed out of the room with his hand on the 9 in his pocket. He slammed the door behind him and told Big Gee it was time to bounce.

The next morning, Tyrell woke up with the sound of Kanika's voice in his ear.

"Tyrell?"

Tyrell opened his eyes in a flash. "What?" he bounced up from the bed.

Kanika looked at him, amused. "What happened to you? This whole room smells like a damn Henny party. Your breath still stinks."

Tyrell brought his hand to his mouth and breathed into it. He *did* smell. "You just got in?" he asked her.

"Did you?" Kanika looked at the shoes he was still wearing.

Tyrell exhaled. He remembered nothing, but that he had been in bed with Tiffany. He couldn't make out the details. He remembered only that his pants were down. He couldn't tell Kanika. "I been home—I was just mad tired. But now I got you back," he said, pulling her down to him.

Kanika lay beside him. He put his arms around her and held her. "I missed you," he said, sticking his nose into her sweet-smelling hair. "How's Little T?"

"He is so good with Ms. Smith. Every moment, he is smiling. He's such a happy baby. He's eating and sleeping well. I doubt he'll forget I'm his mommy."

"Did he mention his *papi*?"

"He did say 'Daddy' a few times."

Tyrell liked that. "Listen, from now on, whatever happens, I don't want you ever leaving me again. We gotta just stay together, no matter what."

Kanika made a little laugh. "You missed me that much, huh?"

"You don't want to know."

Chapter 21

Tiffany had had it all planned: She had heard about Suave's party through friends in Virginia Beach. He was supposed to be big one day and hailed from Brooklyn. Through Rasheeda's network, Tiffany was able to get to the party without a problem and blend in all night without being noticed. She had seen Tyrell the moment he walked in. She expected him to resist her, but not as much as he had. She thought he'd at least let her suck his dick. Kanika was a lucky woman, she thought. She had no doubt Tyrell had mad love for Kanika. But what Kanika didn't know wouldn't hurt her, she thought. Not exactly what Tiffany had in mind.

She rubbed her belly as she fantasized more about Tyrell—his smell, his stance, the way his lips felt. She wanted more, and her little game wasn't over.

"Girl, I would've loved to be a fly on the wall this morning at Tyrell's house," Rasheeda said.

"That nigga probably don't remember shit." Tiffany, lay next to Rasheeda in bed, back home in Virginia. "I do know he has a big dick."

"You saw it?"

"I felt it. Shit, I wish I had that beast in my mouth. I would've sucked his dick so good, he would've fucked me."

"What you gonna do now?"

Tiffany tapped her stomach. "I hope Tyrell saved them baby clothes." She laughed. "When I tell Tyrell that this baby is his, he's gonna beg me to keep the secret. I'll have that nigga on his knees!"

Rasheeda played in Tiffany's hair. "I see I have taught you well."

"Don't we gotta check out your people? We need niggas out here keeping tabs on Tyrell."

"True," Rasheeda said as she slid off the bed in her nakedness.

Tiffany watched Rasheeda's ass bounce from side to side as she walked around the room. "There is some business I wanna take care of."

"You seen his dude Big Gee, right?" Rasheeda asked.

"Yeah, he a'ight."

"If we can get him in our pocket, we can do whatever."

"Not a chance," Tiffany said. "That nigga will lick the crust off Tyrell's shoes. They too close. But I'll worry about that later. If my plan goes well, we won't need anybody's damn help."

Rasheeda got dressed and readied herself to hit the club. "Oh, by the way, I want you to keep this baby, regardless of what happens to Tyrell. I've always wanted to be a mother."

"Huh?" Tiffany said, totally confused.

"Is that a problem?"

"Yes, it's my body. I decide."

"I think you'll see it my way soon enough. I hope it's a little girl," she said, blew a kiss, and left.

Tiffany lay there dumbfounded. She couldn't imagine being a parent with Rasheeda or even letting Rasheeda care for her child.

Where that had suddenly come from scared her. It only proved that Rasheeda had something up her sleeve.

Later that night when Rasheeda returned from the club, Tiffany had some words for her. She was going to make it perfectly clear that she didn't plan to have the baby full-term and had no desire to be anybody's mommy. She was getting tired of Rasheeda running her life, but it was her body, and she wouldn't sit down for anyone.

"Tiffany!" Rasheeda called from the bottom of the stairs.

"I'm over here." Tiffany was sitting in the living room, drinking a glass of Henny.

"Oh, hell no!" Rasheeda said, flying over to grab the glass. "Our baby does not need that."

Tiffany rolled her eyes. "Look—"

"No, you look," Rasheeda said as she rolled her neck. "You think you really slick, don't you?"

"About what?" Tiffany asked, a little nervous.

"I know what happened." Rasheeda moved a few steps closer. "You can never lie to me."

Tiffany turned away. "I have no idea what you sayin'."

"I'm saying you killed Diana!"

Tiffany stopped breathing.

"Did you think you'd get that by me?"

"It was mistake," Tiffany finally said in a casual tone. "She made me do it."

Rasheeda just stood there and glared at Tiffany. It made her feel even worse. "I am sorry I did it. We had a fight, and all of a sudden she was dead—"

"And Lexus helped you with the body?"

Tiffany heard no remorse or sadness in Rasheeda's voice.

"Yeah?" Tiffany said, afraid to look at her.

"Good!" Rasheeda said. She sat down across from Tiffany on the love seat. "Well, you two sure cleaned up good. I would've been so mad if my Persian rug got stained. I would've flipped." She laughed.

Tiffany laughed, too, but it didn't feel right to see Rasheeda laugh. She had thought Rasheeda was in love with Diana.

"I guess I gotta get a new top bitch. Diana was good, but she was getting too hooked on this sweet thing of mine. She didn't wanna work." Rasheeda looked at Tiffany like she'd understand.

"But I thought you two were a couple—"

"Please," Rasheeda said, playing with her hoop earrings. "She was basically my bitch. Did what I wanted, when I wanted, and how I wanted. My little love slave." Rasheeda giggled.

Tiffany wondered about Rasheeda's coldness toward Diana, and if she was next in line for it. If Rasheeda could dispense of Diana like that, what would it be like when it was Tiffany's turn? "I see." Tiffany nodded. "So, I did you a favor?"

"Not exactly, because you owe me. I had love for that bitch. But hey, shit happens. She was one of the only bitches who loved me for me. We went way back. But since I'm gonna be a mommy soon anyway, I need to keep my attention on one thing—you," Rasheeda said, touching Tiffany's slightly bulging belly.

Tiffany flinched.

"Oh, and there's one thing we gotta do."

"What?"

"We need to let Lexus know that his services are no longer needed."

"How?"

"Well, I got somebody else in mind. Lexus has got to go. I don't want him getting no Daddy ideas. You feel me?"

But Tiffany felt sick to her stomach.

———

Around 1 A.M. the next day, Tiffany visited Lexus at his apartment. She kept her 9 close at hand.

"Whatsup?" she said, walking in. She inspected the place with her eyes.

"Looking for something?" he asked, cracking open a can of beer. "Or are you bringing me a raise for getting you all that extra bed in the last few months?"

Tiffany sat on the kitchen counter. "Well, a raise ain't why I'm here. It's about you and me."

Lexus walked in to stand in the gap between her legs. "So you finally starting to fall in love with a nigga?"

"Not exactly," Tiffany said, feeling the metal of his gun up against her thigh. "But I am keeping this baby."

"I told you that was cool with me."

"And me and Rasheeda want to raise it. Actually, Rasheeda wants me to keep the baby for her."

"For who?" he asked, backing away from her.

"Look, I ain't ready to be no mommy. But Rasheeda says she always wanted a kid. So she can have mine."

"How you just gonna give up our shorty like that?"

"So what am I supposed to do? Say no? Rasheeda practically made me. She helped me build the street empire I have. I got connects from here to Memphis because of her. My bank account stays fat. I got the finest clothes, jewels, cars, and home. All because of her. I owe her."

Lexus's eyes turned cold. "I bet if she knew what you did to her girl—"

"She knows, problem solved." Tiffany smirked. "Basically, you just have to get over wanting to be a daddy to this child or wanting to be with me, period."

Lexus nodded. "I'm supposed to work for you and act like I ain't got no kid, even when the kid is here?"

Tiffany yawned. "I need to know you can do that—"

"Or what?"

"Or you're gonna be a problem."

Lexus laughed. "Fuck it, I don't need this shit. I could chill somewhere and be good for years. I got my paper. I don't need you."

Tiffany cocked her gun at him. She just couldn't stand another man leaving her. Anger flowed through her veins.

She hated the person she had become. It was becoming all too easy.

He flexed to get his, and she got him point-blank in the head.

Chapter 22

Kanika had noticed that Tyrell was been acting differently lately. He was spending lots of time at home and keeping somewhat quiet. It occurred to her that maybe something had happened while she was gone.

"So, how much do you miss me?" Kanika asked, lying between his legs as they watched television.

"A lot." He smiled, brushing her cheek with his hand. "I love you."

"I know." Kanika shrugged. "Did something happen while I was gone? Is the spa okay? Did something happen to Big Gee?"

"You know if something went down, I'd have told you. Everything is cool."

"How was that party you went to?"

Tyrell took the remote from her and flipped the channels. "It was wack. You know, a bunch of nobodies trying to be somebody."

Kanika laughed. "So, what does that say about you?"

"I was just trying to show support. You know, bless them with my greatness," he said.

"Oh, really?" Kanika turned her body to face him. His face seemed awfully sad. "Were there a lot of females there?"

"I guess," he said, throwing his hands behind his head to relax. "I was chillin'—"

"Yeah, you better be," Kanika said, and nudged him in the side of his rib cage. "What was Big Gee up to?"

"Same thing. I told you, the party was wack. Wack," he said in frustration. "Now, let's check out this movie here."

"What if there is something else I want to check out?" Kanika said as she pulled on his belt buckle. She unbuttoned his jeans and slipped his dick out through his boxers. "I'm gonna show you how much I missed you."

Tyrell closed his eyes as Kanika lowered her lips to his hardness. She licked it up and down, sucking on it soft and slow. She caressed it with her tongue and lips and inhaled his scent.

"Mmm," Tyrell moaned as Kanika sucked steady and slow. "Damn, I love you—"

Then she stopped.

"Now, are you gonna tell me what happened at the party? I know something happened," Kanika said, waving his dick with her hand as she spoke. "I don't like lies."

Tyrell tucked his dick back in his boxers, still hard and erect. "Nothing happened. I told you. There were chicks there, some were sweating me, a few tried to come on to me."

"Well, that's expected," Kanika said, like it was nothing. "I ain't hating on those bitches. I'm only concerned about you—because if you did something, I will find out. Believe that," Kanika said, and grabbed the remote back.

*K*anika *made* it to the spa the following morning to open the place up. She had rarely opened up, but something told her she needed to get to business bright and early.

"Girl, what are you doing here?" Sheila asked. "Is you trying to take my job?" She laughed while sashaying into the spa with her flowing orange skirt and bright pink top. "You looking cute." Sheila inspected Kanika's high-heeled sandals and shorts.

"Thanks. I just figured I'd get here early, see what I been missing," Kanika said, giving Sheila the eye. She combed her long hair in the mirror and parted it on the side. "Did I miss anything?" Kanika applied glossy red lipstick as she watched Sheila.

Sheila folded a few dried towels from the night before. "Not much. Business still good. The after-school little girl specials are really bringing business. Those little girls are so sweet, the way they sit patiently and wait with their mamas. Of course, they all don't, but—"

"Have you seen Denise?"

"Nah, but she coming in later." Sheila stopped sweeping. "Why, what's going on?" She walked up to Kanika and looked at her suspiciously.

Kanika put her lipstick away. "I need to talk to her about that party Big Gee and Tyrell went to. Something ain't right."

Sheila put the last towel away. "I hope you ain't thinking nothing. You know men will be men, as long as they take care of home."

"Not in my home," Kanika said, putting her hand in the air. "I do not play that. My mother didn't, and neither will I. I ain't gonna be some kept housewife whose husband sticking his dick in everything—" Kanika stopped herself.

"Is that what you thinking of Tyrell?" Sheila put her hand over her mouth. "He would never—"

"Like you said, a man is a man. One thing about Tyrell is that he's never been good at lying to me. I can tell when he acts a certain way."

"What way?"

"This careful, negative, short-on-words way. He said the party was wack. Very negative about it."

Sheila scratched her chin. "Maybe you gotta point." She turned to the door when it opened. "And speak of the devil."

"Hey, ladies," Denise said as she hurried in. "Sorry, I'm a little late. You know the hubby had some unexpected request this morning—"

"Eww, keep your nasty stories to yourself, please," Sheila joked. "Kanika need you to help her out."

"Whatsup, girl?" Denise asked with a concerned look. "I love your heels. Are those Jimmy Choos?"

"Yes," Kanika said with a slight smile. "I'm about to stick these in somebody's ass if I don't get more info about that party Big Gee and Tyrell went to."

"Oh, that party," Denise said, and spun around on her heels back to her station. She started rearranging her curling irons. Both Kanika and Sheila followed her.

"So what you heard?"

"I didn't hear anything, really. Because you know Gee ain't gonna tell me a damn thing. I heard from other people that there were some new-looking people at the party. But no one knows who they were. At least not yet."

"Did they say if Tyrell was with any of them?"

Denise looked at Sheila. "Well, they did say that Tyrell went in this room, and a few minutes later some other chick was in there. But there were a few people in and out of the room. And he went into the room alone."

That satisfied Kanika somewhat, but something told her she needed to do more work. "Denise, find out for me who those 'new' people were. I just have a very bad feeling."

When Kanika got home, Tyrell was there. He was cooking dinner tonight—chicken, sweet potato wedges, and spinach.

He knew one of Kanika's favorite foods was sweet potato wedges.

"You looking good in those shorts," Tyrell said as he tried to place one of the wedges in her mouth. She moved her face away.

"You can stop the act for a minute," she said. "I heard you was at the party and went into a room?"

"Yeah, and?"

"And some chick went in there after you?"

He laughed. "Ain't no chick come after me."

"Tyrell," Kanika said, and turned him around with her hand. "What was you doing in the room?"

"Sleeping." Tyrell fixed his plate and walked out of the kitchen.

"Weren't there some new people at the party?"

"No," he called from the next room. "It was everyone from around the way."

That was when Kanika knew he had lied. Before she went any further with this, she needed more facts.

Chapter 23

Around mid-August, Tiffany found herself in Virginia with a growing belly. Rasheeda was making sure that she was keeping up with her prenatal visits and ordered thousands of dollars of merchandise for the new baby room she was decorating. Tiffany didn't care, because Rasheeda was still taking care of her and giving her free rein over her home and finances.

"All right everyone, this meeting will be quick," Tiffany said in her new office on the other side of town. Rasheeda had rented it for her. She was at the meeting, too, because she wanted to introduce someone new. "Due to some unfortunate circumstances, Lexus won't be with us anymore," Tiffany said, sounding as serious as she could.

"What happened?" asked one of the younger runners, a slim light-skinned kid around seventeen.

"He didn't mind his business just like you," Rasheeda interjected. "Now, fall back and listen."

Tiffany rolled her eyes and continued. "So, though I will miss Lexus, we have a new nigga you all gonna be reporting to." Tiffany looked at Rasheeda, who had found the guy. She herself had never met him.

"This is Blades," Rasheeda said, and opened the door. A six-foot-six, three-hundred-and-fifty-pound man with large hands and dark shades walked in.

Tiffany gulped, and then she smiled to herself because she thought there'd be no problems with being attracted to him. "Blades is gonna be kicking all of you in the ass," Tiffany said. "And reporting to me whoever is fucking up. And whoever is fucking up is gonna get bodied."

A few of the men in the room glanced at each other, as if it had become clear what happened to Lexus.

"Okay, all you muthafuckas can disappear now because we have a party to attend," Rasheeda said. She dismissed everyone with a wave of her hand. She whispered in Tiffany's ear, "So, I'll meet you at Paradise in a few hours. Don't be late, because I have someone else I want you to meet."

W*here's my* bottle?" Tiffany joked as she slid in the booth at the party at about 1 A.M. with Rasheeda, a few guys, and some other females she recognized from the escort service.

Rasheeda had the server pour Tiffany a glass of soda. "So, remember what I told you earlier?"

"Yeah," Tiffany said, and sipped.

"Tonight is special. I'm introducing somebody new to my escort team. She's gonna help me make some serious bread."

Tiffany sipped again and looked around. She didn't see anyone who looked new. But she played it cool. Why Rasheeda needed her to be there, she didn't know.

It wasn't long before Rasheeda was at center stage and ordered the music to stop playing. "Everyone! Muthafuckas! Bitches, hoes, pimps, players, I need your attention," she said, wobbling back and forth on her two high heels while she balanced a slim flute of champagne filled to the brim. "As you know, I keep two people happy in this world—the crackhead and the men who like getting head—"

There were hoots and hollers from several of the men in the crowd, some women, too. "As we celebrate the second anniversary of my little service to humanity, I want to introduce to you the next top bitch. My newest dime. The one that every other bitch is gonna hate—"

Several of the escorts slapped each other fives and rolled their eyes.

"Meet Ruby Red."

A light-skinned, thick, tall, twentyish female jumped up onstage dressed in a see-through black lace bodysuit that shaped her ass to perfection. She hugged Rasheeda and kissed her on the mouth. They stayed embraced as their tongues played with each other.

Everyone clapped and cheered but Tiffany. She was surprised at how much the new girl resembled Diana. Ruby Red looked even better than Diana, she thought. Her heart sank to her knees.

"This is the new top bitch. My bitch," Rasheeda said as her eyes skipped over Tiffany's frozen face.

T*he next* afternoon, Tiffany found Rasheeda and Ruby in the kitchen eating breakfast together like lovebirds.

"Hey, girl," Rasheeda said. She called Tiffany over. "You two didn't have a chance to talk yet."

Tiffany rolled her eyes at Ruby. "Hey," she said dryly.

Ruby smiled back. "So Rasheeda said you two are cousins."

Tiffany shot Rasheeda a look. "Something like that."

"Wow, I wish I had family, but I hope you two will be like my new family. How far are you along?" Ruby glanced at Tiffany's protruding stomach.

"I just lost my appetite," Tiffany said. She slid out of her seat. "I'm going back to bed."

"Hold up," Rasheeda said as she followed Tiffany up the stairs.

Tiffany stopped in her tracks. "So you found a new bitch?"

"Please don't start acting all jealous. We know what happens when you do." Rasheeda manage a small laugh. "It's strictly professional."

"You ain't got to worry about me doing anything that stupid again," Tiffany said, walking to her bedroom.

"Well, there is something I am worried about. It's Lexus," Rasheeda said, standing at the doorway of Tiffany's room.

"He's gone."

"And the feds is on my ass. They in the area now, asking mad questions. You need to bounce."

"Me?"

"Yes, because I'm catching too much heat for what you did. I need to let this pass. It'll take a couple of weeks."

Tiffany twisted her face in anger. "Is it about Lexus or your ho?"

"It's about making sure my baby stays out of harm's way," Rasheeda said. "The baby inside of you."

"And you think I'm safe in New York?"

"I got some people who can look out for you. You was planning on going back anyway, right? You still need to finish business with Tyrell."

That was true, Tiffany thought. She had planned to leave in a few days. But she had a feeling this wasn't about Lexus; it was all about Rasheeda getting her private time. "Fine, I'm out," Tiffany said as she lay down on the bed.

"And you better not think of doing anything to that baby, because I *will* destroy you."

Chapter 24

Yo, I think we need to move on them niggas real soon," Big Gee said to Tyrell in the office below the barber-shop.

"Last time, we flexed on those Colombians, mad niggas got bodied. It cost too much money. We need to just keep doing what we do. We need to take over, expand our shit farther than theirs if we have to. Annihilate those niggas with green blood."

"As far as Virginia?"

"If we have to," Tyrell said, liking the idea the more he thought about it.

"Sounds like you using some of ole Tony's tricks—falling back on the violence?"

Tyrell rocked back and forth in his chair. "Maybe, you know, I learned that I made some mistakes. It had to be done then, but it don't have to be done again."

"True that," said Big Gee. He nodded and rubbed his belly. "I got your back. Now, I'ma get me something to eat. Wanna bounce?"

"I don't know. Kanika may be cooking tonight," Tyrell said as he checked his cell.

"You runnin' home to wifey now?" laughed Big Gee.

"Hold on." Tyrell pulled out his cell to see more clearly who was calling him. "Yo, I think I got some other business to take care of," Tyrell said, hopping out of the chair and giving Big Gee a pound. He flew out of the barbershop and into his ride.

Tiffany wanted to see him. She didn't say what it was about, only that she was in town. It had been a few months since the incident at the party. But Tyrell thought this would be a perfect chance to tell her to fall back and put the fear of God in her. However, there was something about her message that made him think it was urgent. Kanika came to mind, too. He wondered if the bitch had found out where they lived.

"You all right?" Tyrell asked when he heard Kanika's voice on the line.

"Yeah, I'm here waiting for you—"

"Oh, I gotta make a stop. Keep the food warm," Tyrell said, knowing Kanika would be upset.

"That ain't the only thing I'll be keeping warm," Kanika said, and hung up.

Tyrell squeezed the phone in his hand. If Kanika ever found out that Tiffany was at the party, she'd flip. What made it worse, he couldn't remember all the details of what went down. That was what angered him the most. But what Tiffany could possibly want or need wasn't even important. He planned to make sure she got the message never to fuck with him again.

Tyrell met Tiffany at Junior's restaurant in downtown Brooklyn. It was a high-profile place, where it was easy to be seen together. He pulled his baseball cap over his eyes and walked to the back of the restaurant. As he walked by, he must've seen three people he knew. But thankfully, he thought, they didn't see him.

"Why you choose this place?" Tyrell hissed as he sat down across from Tiffany.

"It's a diner, it's downtown. It's close by. Don't make this about you," she said, calmly chewing on the bunch of fries she'd stuffed in her mouth.

"It's my backyard. I can't be out like this with you. Why am I here, anyway?" Tyrell glanced at his watch. "Make it quick."

"Uh." Tiffany giggled as she cleaned her hands with the napkin. "You may want to stick around for this one."

Tyrell leaned across the table. "Stick around for what?"

"Well, where should I begin? Let's see—"

Tyrell reached across the table and grabbed Tiffany by the collar of her white blouse. "Talk, bitch," he said, through his teeth. He let her go.

Tiffany playfully fanned herself as she caught her breath. "I like it rough, but you may want to be careful how you treat me."

"What are you talkin' bout?" he asked. "Yo, I'm out." He stood up.

"Sit down," Tiffany demanded. "It's about what happened between us."

"Ain't nothing happen," Tyrell said as confidently as he could.

"We had sex."

"We didn't."

"You don't remember when we layed down and I was on top of you? You don't remember having your pants down?"

Tyrell's mind raced. He remembered that, but not what happened in between. "That's all that happened."

"There's more," Tiffany said. She slowly rose from the table and put her hand on her belly. "I'm pregnant."

Tyrell stared at Tiffany's stomach, mystified. He bore his eyes into her belly like he wanted to see what was inside. He needed proof, he thought. But the proof was before him, wasn't it.

Frustrated at his silence, Tiffany said, "Well?" as she swung her body back and forth. "Your little son may have a little sister to play with—"

Tyrell's mind faded as Tiffany kept talking. All he could think of was Kanika and how he would tell her. *Kanika.* "How I know it's mine?"

"Because we fucked, that's how!" Tiffany shouted as several patrons look in their direction.

"That ain't enough," he said, working to remain cool.

"I am two months pregnant, and you was the last man. But you know how I really know?"

Tyrell kept his mouth closed.

"Because I planned this. I wanted this to happen. Because this will destroy Kanika more than any gun or weapon." Tiffany grinned. "Am I wrong?"

Tyrell's eyes felt heavy. He didn't want to blink, in case a tear fell. He really fucked up, he thought. It was over. Tyrell stood up to leave.

Tiffany grabbed him by his arm. "I'm gonna tell her," she said. "Or will you?"

Tyrell yanked his arm back and bounced. He had to tell Kanika because there was no way around this one.

At **midnight,** Tyrell finally came home. He thought maybe he could let tonight slide while he mulled it over in bed and rehearsed what to say. But when he unlocked the door, Kanika was dressed from head to toe in Victoria's Secret.

"What took you so long?" she asked. "I told you I'd try to keep it warm."

Tyrell's eyes moved all over Kanika's fit, curvy body in a pink-and-black corset and garter. Her hair was flipped over her shoulder, and she had glossy red lips. He wanted to taste her mouth.

"Come here," she said, calling him over with her finger. She tackled him onto the bed, rubbing her body against his. "I wanna eat you up tonight."

Tyrell tried to rise to the occasion but couldn't.

"What's wrong?" Kanika asked. Her face looked like she was about to burst into tears. "You not rejecting me, are you?"

"No, no," he said, pulling her back down on him. "I'm just tired."

"Well." She slipped his hand inside her warm panties. "You feel this. It's wet, it's hot, it needs to be fucked. So, you just lay back and let me ride."

He still couldn't do it.

Kanika traced his lips with her tongue and kissed him from his neck to his navel. She unbuttoned his shirt and slipped down his pants and boxers.

"Wow, I never seen you like this," she said, holding his limp dick. "Tell me what happened."

Tyrell rolled off the bed. "It's Tiffany."

"Tiffany who?"

"Your half sister. Crazy-ass Tiffany."

Kanika took in a deep breath. "What?"

"Remember that party—?"

"Yeah, I remember, nigga!" Kanika said, flying into his face. "I knew that bitch was there."

"So, uhm, what happened was that—"

Kanika slapped him cold in the face.

Tyrell held his jaw; a small stream of blood came from the side of his mouth. She had slapped him so hard, he bit his tongue.

"Say it!" she demanded. "And skip the specifics."

Tyrell licked the blood from his mouth as his chest caved in. He sat down and covered his face in his hands.

Kanika stood lifeless. She had never seen him this distraught unless one of his boys died.

"She said she's pregnant with my child."

Kanika almost fainted. She held the side of the bed for support when her knees gave out. "You fucked her?"

"I swear I didn't. I know I didn't."

"Then how is she pregnant?"

Kanika's voice was strangely low. It made him even more nervous. "I just can't remember everything. But I know that baby can't be mine."

Kanika grabbed her luggage out of the closet as she dropped whatever she could find in it. "I know I did this before, but this time it's for good."

"Hold up," Tyrell said, snatching the clothes from her.

She pointed at his face. "Don't you ever come around me and Little T again. I will have you killed. Don't fuck with me!" Kanika exploded.

Tyrell took a few steps back and watched her dash around the room in a fury.

"We shouldn't even be having this conversation. We shouldn't even be talking about Tiffany!" she said, throwing some clothes at him. "You killed me the first time when you told me about my mother's death, but this is the last time."

Tyrell's eyes got wet. He wanted to stop her, but it was too late. She was right, he thought. Whether Tiffany was pregnant with his child or not wasn't so important as why she was there in the room that night with him. Tyrell knew he couldn't get Kanika back right away, but he had to at least get Tiffany to admit the truth.

Chapter 25

Tiffany wasn't getting used to sleeping alone. Ruby Red was coming by at least twice a week and spending lots of time with Rasheeda. Tiffany had heard them a few times in Rasheeda's room. She still wasn't sure what kind of role Ruby Red filled for Rasheeda, besides being the newest escort. But things did get a little easier to deal with, since Rasheeda was including her in activities she and Ruby Red had planned.

Today they were going to the beach. The warm September weather provided a nice backdrop with the calm water and clear blue skies. A typical Saturday, the beach was packed, so Rasheeda and Ruby Red laid their blankets down in a more secluded area of the beach. Rasheeda supplied the weed and cognac with Coke, but passed on Tiffany.

"Girl, I didn't know you had it like that," Ruby Red said to Tiffany as she unhooked her bra to join Rasheeda and Ruby Red, who had done the same.

Tiffany cupped her big brown breasts in her hand. "You don't, but someone else does," she said, winking at Rasheeda, who had already lain back on her beach chair.

Ruby Red struggled to keep her smile intact.

Tiffany slipped in the chair between Ruby Red and Rasheeda and turned on the small boom box they had brought with them. "Ooh, that is my song," Rasheeda said, snapping her fingers.

"That is so old-school." Ruby Red laughed as she listened to the Cameo song.

"How old are you?" Tiffany asked her.

"Twenty-two," Ruby Red said proudly. "I am far too young for those songs," she said, moving her chair closer to Rasheeda.

Tiffany thought that was a bold move, but she let it slide.

The three of them enjoyed the sun and the music for about an hour until Rasheeda and Ruby Red ventured into the water.

Tiffany watched from afar as they splashed each other and their bodies touched amid the waves. Rasheeda seemed to be finger-fucking Ruby Red, who made enough faces that Tiffany lost count. Ruby Red put her arms around Rasheeda's neck as the two did their thing.

Tiffany snuck a cigarette and a cup of Henny and Coke before Rasheeda got back. She knew if she saw it, she'd flip.

"Whew! The water is nice," Rasheeda said as she began to dry her body off with the towel.

"I'm sure it was very nice." Tiffany flashed a sarcastic smile as she looked straight ahead into the ocean.

Just then few men walked in their direction while Rasheeda and Ruby Red dried each other off.

"Excuse me, is that Rasheeda Williams?" asked one of the men, a short muscular guy with sneakers and shorts on.

"Hey, Mr. Man!" Rasheeda went up to the men and put her arm around one of them. "Y'all, I want you to meet Scottie. This is my boy from way back in high school."

Tiffany gave a faint wave, as did Ruby Red, while Scottie's boys' mouths watered at all the thigh and legs before them.

"Some things don't change—you still get all the ladies." Scottie laughed.

Rasheeda did, too. "This is my newest lady, and hopefully my last. Ruby Red."

Tiffany watched Ruby Red hop up and greet the fellas with a hug, lingering too long on some, she thought. Ruby Red was officially Rasheeda's new girlfriend. So what did that mean for her? She already felt ousted. Rasheeda hadn't even bothered introducing her.

As the men walked away, Tiffany ignored what had just happened. She played it cool while Rasheeda and Ruby Red acted like lovebirds. Until Rasheeda said, "Oh, and I got your plane ticket to NY. Got it all hooked up. You are leaving tomorrow."

*R*asheeda had set Tiffany up with an apartment at a discreet location in downtown Brooklyn. She was living in the projects on Myrtle Avenue. It wasn't exactly what Tiffany would have chosen, but it was close enough to Tyrell's business. She was staying with another one of Rasheeda's friends, Misa, who was never home, because of her night job as a home attendant. Tiffany and Misa didn't talk much, but all Tiffany needed from her were the places to be and when.

"So, girl, what are you gonna do about that baby?" Misa asked a couple of nights later as she walked in on Tiffany in the kitchen.

"Keep eatin'," Tiffany said, and stuffed a spoonful of pistachio ice cream in her mouth. "Until the baby daddy fess up."

"You never told me who it was."

"Tyrell, *the* Tyrell," Tiffany said with a sly grin.

"No, girl! Oh my God. Isn't he married to—?"

"So what? He fucks."

"Obviously, he ain't fucking only his wife—"

"She ain't his wife," Tiffany said, throwing her spoon in the sink.

Misa flinched at Tiffany's anger. "I mean, don't he go with Kanika? She is beautiful. I heard what happened to her people—"

"Things change," Tiffany said as she brushed past Misa. She wasn't really feeling her questioning. "Anyway, he's the father of this baby. Actually, he and I may even end up together."

"You and Tyrell? He is like the number one nigga around here. Every bitch wants him. How'd you do it?"

"That's my secret. But once he got a whiff of this pussy, it was all over," Tiffany said, crossing her legs. "I just need to get the word out."

Misa laughed. "I know I would! Having a baby for a nigga like that. Everyone should know about it by now."

"Everyone *will* know."

"Honey, if you told me, best believe that I will carry the message far and wide. Just tell me one thing: Was it good?"

"It was better than good. He made love to me. He touched every inch of this body," Tiffany said, jutting out her hips.

"Are you two *together* together?"

"Oh, I'm working on it, but don't get no fuckin' ideas."

At around 6 A.M., Tiffany awoke with one of the wildest ideas she'd had in a while. Instead of waiting for all of Brooklyn to find out, she wanted to tell the main person who needed to know directly. While Misa was at work, Tiffany hurried and got dressed.

A few hours later, she arrived at Kanika's apartment building.

When she saw the security guard busy with a FedEx carrier, she snuck in on the heels of an elderly woman.

The elderly white woman in her seventies wearing a black sweater and red handkerchief gave Tiffany the eye. She stood very close to the elevator door.

"Excuse me, ma'am," Tiffany asked. "Do you know of a Tyrell or Kanika in this building?"

"A clinic?" asked the elderly woman when she turned around.

Tiffany rolled her eyes. "No—*Kanika*. Do you know of anyone by that name?"

The woman turned back around to face the elevator door.

Tiffany thought what else she might ask to get the info she needed. "Where do the black people live?"

That caught the elderly woman's attention. She opened her tight round mouth and said, "There's not many in this building."

"I know, so the ones who are, where do they live?"

"Well, there's a very nice young black couple on the twenty-second floor. Are you here for them?"

The elevator door opened to the elderly woman's floor.

"Yes, I am. But I don't have the exact apartment number."

The elderly woman smiled. "It's 22E."

The door closed, and Tiffany pressed the elevator to go up to the twenty-second floor. When she got off, she saw the apartment immediately and went over to ring the bell.

But no one answered. She rang again.

Tiffany took out her little equipment box that had all the tools to bust open any lock. She felt her mind spinning as she tried to get the lock open. A rush of adrenaline caused her to jam it in several times until the door unlocked.

"Hello?" Tiffany whispered into the empty apartment. "Hello?"

She walked into the many rooms and saw no one. She put her hands on her hips and thought that maybe Kanika had left but would be back soon. If that was the case, she wanted to make the most of her time there. She found Kanika's walk-in closet that housed walls of designer shoes, handbags, jeans, dresses, and expensive belts and accessories. She inhaled the citrusy floral scent of the clothes and lost herself in it. She rubbed a luxurious mink-cropped jacket against her face, then slipped it on. She walked through the racks and found a leather halter top with a lace front. She tried that on, too. Then a pair of jeans that were too small, a pair of leopard-print Christian Louboutins, and a thick braided Versace belt.

She became Kanika for a moment. She skipped around the room, wearing her half sister's clothes and posed in the mirror. She thought she looked almost as beautiful as Kanika. She spotted Kanika's lingerie drawer and rummaged through her cotton and lace panties, bras, and nighties. She stuffed several in her bag. Perhaps, she thought, she could be like Kanika, and then Tyrell would want her. She applied Kanika's signature red lipstick to her lips and dabbed on dots of eyeshadow and blush. She combed her short hair to the side, like Kanika often kept her own hair. Taking a final look in the mirror, Tiffany felt nothing looking like Kanika, and left.

Chapter 26

He is growing up so fast," Kanika said as she held Little T in her arms. "I can't help but think of his daddy when I look into that tiny little face."

"Well, you don't have to think about his daddy. You can call him." Ms. Smith handed Kanika the warmed baby bottle. "It's been two weeks so far."

"I know," Kanika said as she inserted the nipple of the bottle into Little T's mouth. "I guess at some point I have to take his calls."

"Absolutely," Ms. Smith urged. "I heard the whole story, and dear, I feel for you. I know how it is to have a man betray you, but your story sounds like there must be more to it."

"Like what?"

"I think you really need to sit down with your half sister and clear the air. Get the truth. Something is missing."

Kanika laughed. "You talk like me and my half sister can stand each other. I hate her, and she hates me, too. The only time you'd find us in the same room would be if one of us was holding a piece of metal to the head."

"Huh?" Ms. Smith said.

"I mean we'd be trying to kill each other. Really, Ms. Smith, I know you're trying to help, but I gotta do this my way. I can't just call Tiffany—"

"Your way is what? To get the whole story, you have to reach out to her somehow."

"I got the whole story from Tyrell."

"I think not," Ms. Smith said, folding her arms. "This is your family we are talking about. We are talking about not just your husband messing up, but the future of your little son, your future. Are you gonna let some rumors or misunderstandings destroy that?"

"Are you saying I should run back?"

"No, but get all the facts. Stand up to Tiffany—at whatever cost."

Kanika dabbed the moisture from Little T's lips and gave him to Ms. Smith. She stood at the window, pulled back the red-and-yellow curtains, and looked out at the home that used to be hers. "You know, Ms. Smith. I'm just scared. I've lost so much, I'm just afraid if I really lose it, I'll hurt somebody. I can kill someone. I have to think about Little T."

Ms. Smith smiled. "I understand. How about you start at square one? Start by taking Tyrell's phone calls. Listen to what the man has to say. You don't have to reply. But when a man is as persistent and consistent as he is, there may be some merit to his words."

"He keeps saying the baby ain't his. He ain't saying they didn't sleep together," Kanika said.

"But he said he can't remember. I believe him. Who knows what kind of lies that child is drumming up? Are you gonna believe her over your husband?"

"Tiffany would do whatever she could to destroy me. She

wouldn't miss the chance of sleeping with Tyrell. Not at all,"
Kanika said in an insistent tone.

W *hen Tyrell* returned to the apartment later that evening,
he immediately sensed that someone had been there. The
door was unlocked. Clothes were scattered on the ground. There
were panties on the doorknob. He wondered why Kanika hadn't
used her keys. But then he caught a scent in the apartment that
signaled to him that somebody entirely new had been there.
Kanika's scent was gone.

Tyrell pulled out his gun and walked softly from room to
room. *Love, Tiffany* was written on the bedroom mirror in one of
Kanika's lipsticks.

Tyrell opened every door, even the cabinets. He wasn't putting anything past her. But there was no sign of her.

He dialed Big Gee. "That VA bitch Tiffany was in my crib. I want
niggas to go down there and do some work. Find out her people
and come back with some connects. I got a plan to take over that
bitch territory. I think she's planning to push her way up here."

"Word," Big Gee said on the other end. "I heard some of her
people was up here, asking about you. They was acting like they
wanted to make amends, but nah. Where Kanika at?"

"She's Upstate. I don't know what that bitch Tiffany trying to
do breaking into my goddamn house. If Kanika was here, Tiffany
woulda been a dead bitch."

"Need me to come by?"

"Nah, I need to take over that bitch's shit before she do me in.
You know we going through a little change here and there, and I
don't need no out-of-town niggas looking at what I got like fresh
territory."

"I got your back, man. I'll send some peoples down there this weekend. See what's up. Yo, we can definitely bust our moves down there, though."

"I know that."

"And yo, what's up with Kanika being Upstate? The girls at the spa was like they hadn't seen her in a minute."

"We going through something."

"Yeah, I feel you, man," Big Gee said.

"Get back to me when it's done, because I'm gonna get them before they get me." Tyrell clicked off his phone and closed his eyes.

On **Thursday** afternoon, Tyrell paid a surprise visit to Kanika and his son. It wasn't a surprise to Ms. Smith, because he had told her to expect him but not let Kanika know. He didn't want to deal with Kanika not wanting to see him or stressing herself out.

When he knocked on the door, the surprise was over. "What are you doing here?" Kanika asked, holding Little T on her hip.

"I came to see you and Little T. Can I come in?"

Kanika stepped to the side, let him in, and closed the door behind Tyrell.

He took Little T from her arms, but Kanika resisted. "No, not until you tell me what you want."

"That's my son," Tyrell said, shocked that she wouldn't give him the baby.

"Seems like you forgot that the night you was with Tiffany. You forgot about me, too," Kanika hissed. "I don't want to argue in Ms. Smith's house. You saw Little T, and now you can leave."

"Kanika," Ms. Smith said, appearing at the top of the steps. She was holding her bag. "I knew Tyrell was coming. I'm going to the market. I can take Little T while you two talk."

Tyrell looked at Kanika, who cut her eyes at Ms. Smith. Kanika handed the baby to Ms. Smith, and went to the living room with Tyrell.

When Kanika heard the front door shut, she went off. "Now you can get the fuck out!" she said, jumping out of the chair. "I really don't want to have to repeat myself."

Tyrell stayed seated. He held his hands tightly together to remain calm because he knew Kanika was going to press all his buttons. "Sit down," he told her. "All I need is twenty minutes."

"Make it five," Kanika said, tapping her foot and refusing to sit.

"I want you to come home. All this going on between us can be worked out if we see each other and work through this shit."

"Tyrell, I would rather you had sex with some skank I didn't know than Tiffany. That was the ultimate disrespect you could do to me."

Tyrell stood up. "I didn't have sex with her. I mean, I don't think I did." He grabbed her by the shoulder. "I love you. You gotta believe me."

She shrugged out of his hold. "I don't have to do anything but take care of me and Little T. I can't trust you. What we had was built on trust. What am I supposed to do now?"

"Love me."

"I hate you, Tyrell. I could never love you like I did."

Tyrell rubbed his forehead. "Look, I don't know what the fuck to do! I need you home. You my wife. Start acting like it!"

"Hell no!" Kanika said as she rolled her neck. "You gotta start acting like a husband first. You really have some goddamn nerve. I think your five minutes are up," she said, walking to the door.

He didn't move.

"Tyrell!" Kanika called.

He didn't answer.

She marched back into the living room. "I swear if this was my house, all of this shit would be on the floor now. I need you to get the hell out."

"So you never coming back home?"

"I don't know."

"I guess you don't care about how many other females would fight to be in your shoes right now," Tyrell said, hurt by Kanika's shutting him down.

"I'm sure you do," Kanika said, and she rolled her eyes.

"Fuck it!" He threw his hands in the air and walked quickly to the front door. "I see you ain't never gonna listen to me until I prove you wrong."

"I could listen to you—it doesn't mean I have to believe you. Until I can trust you again, I may never come home."

Chapter 27

T iffany didn't think she could do it, but she did. After a couple of phone calls, she was able to get her people to ambush Tyrell's crew in Jamaica, Queens. Now she owned a little piece of Tyrell's empire.

She lay in bed at Misa's apartment and listened to all the messages on her cell. The blood. The glory. It was still early, around 5 A.M., so word hadn't spread yet. But Tiffany knew Tyrell already knew—or was about to. All she wanted was to see the look on his face.

"Rasheeda, I did something you'd be proud of," Tiffany boasted on the phone.

"I'm listening."

"Well, I got a few of my VA people to do Tyrell and his crew in up here in Queens. I got a bit of empire."

"You did what!"

"You heard right."

"You didn't tell me."

"Because I just thought of it in the last few days. The nigga already think I got his baby and he don't care—well, I'm gonna make him care. I'ma take over all this."

There was a brief pause; then Rasheeda said with a smile in

her voice, "Girl, that is a bold muthafuckin' move. You sure you ready for what you started?"

"Am I in this alone?"

"No, I told you I'd look out, but—"

"But what?"

"I got my own money to worry about."

"What I did was for us. You can distribute you shit up here. What I have, you have."

"I have my hands full from here to Memphis. Don't get me wrong—you did a slick-ass move—but now you gotta finish what you started."

"Oh, this is nothing. I ain't stopping until I get Brooklyn and have that nigga Tyrell on his knees with that bitch Kanika. She's next on my list."

"I swear, you are just like your daddy. I ain't mad at you. Let me think what I can do. I certainly ain't one to turn a blind eye to some extra bread."

"Definitely not," Tiffany said. "Unless you getting soft now because you got a new woman."

"This ain't got nothing to do with that. I'm just trying to be smart about it. Remember what happened the last time we pissed Tyrell off."

Tiffany nodded to herself.

"But let me see. Shit, maybe I'll help you take over his Brooklyn spot. Gotta talk to my people, though. You know?"

"I know that you are the head bitch in charge. Who else needs to know?"

"Let me put it this way: To take over a nigga like Tyrell, you gotta kill him. If I can't have it all, I don't want jack."

"That's whatsup. I got a call in to him today. I just wanna hear it in his voice. He's gonna wish he never met Kanika, and that means he would've never met *me*."

---

*B*y **midafternoon,** Tiffany's phone was blowing up at a new level. She hadn't left the house, and didn't plan to for a few days.

Tiffany looked through the peephole of the apartment when the bell rang. Two cops flashed their IDs.

"This is the FBI. We have a few questions for Tiffany," said one of the officers.

Tiffany pressed her back against the door. The first thought that came to her mind was that her Queens shutdown of Tyrell had come back to bite her in the ass. But she was no chump. She had seen her father stand up to the police before. He never let them see him sweat.

"Officers?" Tiffany said as she parted the door slightly. "What can I do for you?"

"Can we come in?" said, a tall red-haired officer still holding up his badge. He was accompanied by another officer.

"Sure." Tiffany stepped aside. "By the way, can we make this quick? I have a hair appointment."

"Well, ma'am, we got word that you may know something about the disappearance of Diana Williams. Do you?"

"Diana Williams?" Tiffany looked up at the ceiling like she was trying to remember. "Wasn't she a prostitute?"

"She was an escort or a dancer. We're still trying to piece this together," said the other officer. His thick bifocal glasses rested on the tip of his nose.

"I heard she was a prostitute and had some problems with a john or something." Tiffany checked her cell phone, like she had better things to do. "Anything else?"

"How did you know her?" asked the red-haired one.

Tiffany kept her eyes on her cell phone, then looked up. "Through a friend. I think I met her at a party."

"Party?"

"Yes, I really don't know her. I wish I could be of more help."

But the officers didn't move to leave.

"Are we done?" Tiffany asked.

"Here's our card. If anything else comes to mind, give us a call," said the red-haired officer.

"Actually, how did you get my information?"

"I'm sorry, ma'am. We can't reveal that," he said. "We just have our ways. Good day."

With that, the officers left. But Tiffany was starting to panic. Rasheeda could have leaked some anonymous tip to the cops, she thought. She was the only one Tiffany had told besides Lexus. She ripped up the cop's card as anger rose inside her. The last thing she needed was Diana's case making her hot while she was starting to make big moves.

That night, Tiffany couldn't sleep. She tossed and turned in the bed, afraid to let her guard down. She had expected to feel this way, but the cops coming to her door threw her off completely. Misa came home at her usual midnight hour, but this time she wasn't alone.

Tiffany listened as Misa was out in the living room with a guy. She could hear his deep laughter and masculine grunts as they watched television together. Tiffany was curious about how he looked. It had been a minute since she felt the arms of any man around her and he wasn't trying to choke her out. She put her hand on her belly and noticed that her baby bump was a slight pooch. She wondered if she still had it going on with the fellas.

"Damn, you two are loud for no reason," Tiffany said as she strolled into the living room in shorts and a tank top. Misa's man looked like a tasty treat. "Hello." Tiffany shook his hand.

"How you doing? I'm ShaDarrius, but people call me Sha," he said as he shook her hand tight and quick. Tiffany felt Misa's eyes on her. Tiffany knew her thick thighs and shapely ass had Misa's man sweating her instantly.

"Tiffany is just staying with me for a minute," Misa said. ShaDarrius kept his eyes on Tiffany. "Tiffany, are we keeping you up?" her roommate asked

"Not at all," she said, sitting directly across from ShaDarrius. "I'm bored as shit. Anybody got some weed? I can't sleep."

"We don't smoke that anymore," Misa said, taking ShaDarrius's hand. "Ain't that right?"

"Yeah, I mean, I used to." ShaDarrius laughed nervously.

Misa shook her head, a bit frustrated. "I'm gonna pack a little bag to take to ShaDarrius's apartment. So you'll have the place all to yourself," Misa said, getting up to walk to her bedroom.

Tiffany and ShaDarrius sat awkwardly as they both focused on the news—or acted like it. Tiffany figured she didn't have long to make a move. She was bored, and Misa should've known better.

Tiffany slipped beside him on the couch, her thigh touching his. "You got really nice hair," she said, tracing her curling hairline with her finger. "Are you mixed?"

"My mom is Spanish, my father is black," ShaDarrius said, his eyes jumping from Tiffany's legs to her big breasts that pressed against her tank.

"Nice." Tiffany let her hand fall down to his chest. "I don't have any Spanish in me, but I want to." She put her hand on his jeans zipper.

"Uhm—" ShaDarrius's body stiffened.

"It'll only take a minute. She's gonna be in there for a while." Tiffany unzipped his jeans.

ShaDarrius opened his legs wider and stuck his neck out for Misa. Then he grinned.

Tiffany pulled ShaDarrius's firm dick out of his drawers and licked it.

ShaDarrius jutted his hips out as she licked and sucked some more. Tiffany took pleasure in sucking him. He was a perfect stranger, and she got off on that real bad. Her pussy throbbed as she sucked him hard and fast.

Then she noticed ShaDarrius's dick softening. She looked up and saw Misa standing there with her handbag, like a mannequin.

"My bad," Tiffany said with a nervous giggle. "I was just looking for some spare change I dropped down there." She wiped her mouth off and looked at Misa, who couldn't do a thing. Misa knew Tiffany wasn't one to play with or have on her bad side.

"I—I—" Misa stuttered with fear in her eyes, looking at Sha-Darrius, who was already zipped up and sitting pretty.

"She's right, baby, uh, it's not what it looks like."

Tiffany made a fake yawn. "I think I'll go to bed now," she said, brushing shoulder to shoulder with Misa.

Chapter 28

Tyrell didn't know *what* hit him. But he didn't have to know in order to be prepared. It was clear to him that Tiffany wanted more than just him but to take over his territory and completely destroy his and Kanika's lives.

"Yo," Tyrell said as he picked up his phone in the office. "Big Gee—"

"Yeah, man, I got Mike. Before he split the nigga head open for good, I got him to show us who Rasheeda and Tiffany working with. Rasheeda is a distributor, but she gets her shit from some Mexican niggas. So, I had a little meeting with them. They down with giving us some product at a good price, better than we had with the Colombians up here. We can bust a move in VA any day."

"They willing to give us a piece of that VA pie? I want to take over Tiffany. If it mean taking over that bitch Rasheeda, too, let's do it."

"No question. By the end of the day, what Tiffany did to us is gonna be multiplied two or three times down there. We about to shut niggas down today."

The call ended. Tyrell thought all he had to do was wait a

few hours and he'd get another call about the results. He liked being number one. He remembered the days when he was the one on the streets carrying out the orders by the other big dogs. When he finally took over Tiffany, he'd be even bigger and more powerful. He fantasized about moving even farther away with Kanika and his son. He wanted to be in the game, but he didn't want to live the game like he was doing now. He wanted to be removed from it and be a family man and be the best husband to Kanika.

About five hours later, the call came. It was Big Gee.

"Well?" Tyrell asked as soon as he picked up.

"It was crazy. We came up on them niggas and rushed like ten crews out of Virginia Beach. I mean tens of tens of niggas who claimed to be working with Tiffany. We stole their product. We took over them niggas. To make a long story short, the streets is really quiet tonight down here. All you can see is bloodstains on the walls."

"And Tiffany?"

"Her ass must still be in New York. We went as far as Rasheeda's crib, but bitch got some new type security that keep strangers like at a three-mile radius or an alarm goes off. You need some code or some shit. But we hit them in their pocket. Where it hurts."

Tyrell smiled. "I bet them bitches didn't think I had the fuckin' nerve, but they messed with the wrong nigga. And I ain't finished till I take over the whole of VA. Take all that ho bread. Have them out in the streets."

"Word." Big Gee laughed. "The carnage has only begun."

"Holla at me later," Tyrell said, and hung up. This was the beginning of something big, which could either take his reign to a new level or destroy everything he'd worked for. He was more than willing to risk it all for Kanika.

S*heila went* to visit Kanika and tell her about the news. As soon as Kanika saw Sheila and the look on her face, she knew something bad was up.

Sheila put her arms around her when she saw Kanika at the door. "I missed you, girl. You just totally forgot about us, huh?"

"Not at all." Kanika led Sheila to the living room where Little T was asleep in his playpen.

"Oooh, he is the cutest thing. Got Tyrell's eyebrows," Sheila said, peeking over the playpen.

"And his nose, and his lips," Kanika chimed in. "I tried to get away from him even for a little while, and he still manages to be in my face every day."

"Where's the lady you stay with?"

"She's at church. Ms. Smith has really been an angel to me." Kanika poured two glasses of orange juice from the pitcher. "To what do I owe this little surprise visit?"

"I guess you haven't heard," Sheila said, her face turning long.

Kanika put her manicured hands over her glass and sipped. "Heard what? I heard everything I needed to know. Tyrell played me."

"Girl, let me tell you, whatever happened between the two of you is taking a toll on him. That bitch Tiffany y'all got beef with took over a spot of his in Queens last week. Then I heard earlier that Tyrell and his crew massacred Tiffany's VA crew. He wants to expand into her area."

The orange juice suddenly tasted bad to Kanika. Tyrell always confided in her about any move he wanted to make. She was the first to know. But lately, she thought, she hadn't been the easiest person to talk to. "He is okay, right?"

"Of course, girl. How long has it been since you spoke to him?"

"A few weeks." Kanika felt a rush of tears coming. "I swear if anything ever happened to him—"

Sheila put her hand on Kanika's shoulder. "Nothing happened to him. You two need to nip this in the bud."

"He got somebody pregnant."

"How do you know for sure?"

"Because he's actin' guilty."

"Girl, no. He's trying to prove to you that the bitch is evil. He's trying to get rid of her. You gotta think that through."

"I don't know for sure, Sheila."

"I understand. I'm not saying go back home now. Get all the facts before you do. But understand that Tyrell loves you. He'll do anything for you."

Kanika thought that Tyrell shouldn't be going through what he was doing alone. "I think I need to handle Tiffany woman to woman. We got a lot of unfinished businesses. I'm not gonna let her fuck with Tyrell or me, but she is carrying his child."

"Exactly! And I know where that bitch is stayin'."

"Yeah, but that child she has is his child, too. I can't just ignore Tiffany—she's gonna be a part of my life whether I like it or not, some way or another. I need to think through this because I don't wanna fuck up what Tyrell is doing. I also don't want him to think he is getting off easy."

By the next morning, Kanika was in Brooklyn. It was dangerous territory, with everything that had gone down. But she needed to talk to Tyrell, and she knew where to find him.

When she walked into the barbershop, all eyes were on her. She looked straight ahead, her eyes shielded by her black Dior shades as Big Gee led her downstairs to Tyrell.

The large metal basement door opened, and her eyes zoomed in on him. He was seated at his desk with the cell to his ear. As soon as he saw her, he handed the call to Big Gee, who left them alone.

"I guess you heard?" Tyrell asked as he stood up.

"You can sit down," Kanika said, sitting herself on a chair. "Are you okay?"

Tyrell offered a satisfied smile. "I'll be okay when you come home."

"Look," Kanika said, adjusting her shades on her face. "I really came to talk about what went down. We usually talk about big moves like that. You trying to take over VA?"

"I already started," Tyrell said as he sat down. "I actually plan to make Tiffany disappear period."

"She got your baby—"

"It ain't mine—"

Kanika waved at the air like she didn't want to get into it. "Anyway, I remember Tony was always wary about doing business down South."

Tyrell held his breath. Then he said, "It's different times now. We gotta go where the money is."

"Well, if you gonna do all that, I need to be a part of it. It's my family business, our family business. You're not the only one calling the shots."

"I call the final shot. Always," he said strongly.

"Listen, I am cool with what went down. I just wanted to know before everyone else did. But I don't want you to think that what you did is gonna make me run back to you. The fact remains that you fucked Tiffany. You still fucked up."

"But I am doing all I can to fix that. Once we have Tiffany out of our lives for good, we can live at peace, or close to it."

Kanika stood up to leave. "Just answer me one question: Did you think of me at all when you were with her?"

"I didn't even know I was with her! Next thing I knew she was on top of me and everything got blurry. I was filled up to my nose with Henny."

"That's the part that scares me. But you remember nothing?" Kanika asked, glad her shades hid her eyes.

"I don't. I just know I want to fix it," he said, walking over and standing close to her. He bent down and went to kiss her lips, but she moved her face away.

"The only one who can fix this is me. No matter what you say. And until then, I ain't coming back. I'm embarrassed and disgusted. Good-bye." Kanika left and slipped into the Escalade that waited for her outside. This time her tears weren't from sadness, but from relief. She still loved him.

Chapter 29

The nigga came out of nowhere!" Tiffany shouted as she and Rasheeda sat amidst the ruins of Club Paradise.

"What did you *think* he would do after that stunt you pulled?" Rasheeda stepped over the charred chairs and tables. It had been set on fire the night before.

"I just didn't think he'd do it like this. I mean, he shut down half of my business already. My money!" Tiffany stomped.

"My money, too. When you lose, I lose twice as hard because I'm the one you get your stuff from. What the hell did you start?"

Tiffany sat down on the ash-filled ground. "I can't believe this! Everybody is gone. Niggas is losing faith in me. How am I gonna get my shit back?"

"You just gonna have to do it. It's either you or the block. Right now, Tyrell's got the block. You ain't got shit."

"I know that, but I also know that there's gotta be a way. I know I can get Tyrell. I took over only a small part of Queens, but he's taken much more from me. That only means one thing."

"What?"

"I gotta make sure I take over his whole shit, bring my force up there to Brooklyn. Blow all his shit up. This is muthafuckin' war. I'm tired of the little fucking battles."

"This is costing me too much money and time. Tyrell definitely has to be dealt with. I say, fuck all the control over this or that, one of you gotta die for this to be completely over."

"It ain't gonna be me," Tiffany said, dusting off her behind. "I got a baby to look after."

Rasheeda rolled her eyes. "And it ain't gonna be me, for damn sure."

"Listen, if we put our heads together, we can take Tyrell out. I need you on this with me, Rasheeda. I know you can make it happen. You plugged in with all the right people."

Rasheeda blew down on her nails as she listened to Tiffany's plea. Then said, "I don't think so."

"Excuse me?" Tiffany asked, feeling like she was hearing things.

"I don't wanna have anything to do with you killing Tyrell or taking over more of his territory. To be honest, what that nigga did to you has showed me what he's working with, and I don't want none of that. Shit, I don't wanna destroy all the possibilities of maybe even making some money with him."

"No, you wouldn't do that," Tiffany said, not believing her ears.

"Hell, I would. Look, I can put aside whatever bullshit for paper, bread, *dinero*. What you think this whole thing is about?"

"Respect, loyalty—"

Rasheeda laughed at Tiffany. "You wouldn't know respect or loyalty if it hit you on the head. Are you saying I'm supposed to feel some loyalty towards you?"

Tiffany didn't answer.

"You made your own bed, you sleep in it," Rasheeda said, and left Tiffany alone in the ruins of Paradise.

A t *about* 11 P.M., Tiffany decided to have a private meeting with her lieutenant, Blades.

"I need you to do me a favor," she said to him as they sat in Roscoe's Chicken and Waffles.

"Whatever you need," he said, stuffing a waffle into his mouth.

"It's Tyrell. I gotta cap that nigga. I need you to find him, kill him, his wife, and his baby. I want pictures, too."

Blades wiped his mouth. "Everybody tryin' to lay low right now after what happened. Niggas don't want no more beef. I think we should fall back at least for a couple of months. Get the business back in order."

"It ain't gonna end with what happened. This is only the start. With Tyrell walking around seeking revenge on me, anything is possible. I ain't taking no chances on him."

Blades pushed his plate away. His large belly stood between him and the table. "I don't know."

"I'm giving you an order," Tiffany said, flailing her finger in the air. "You have no choice."

"I'm supposed to look after things and make sure niggas don't trip. I make sure that your money is right and that niggas is out there hustling. To me, that is what matters. And yeah, I'd cap a nigga in a minute, if it's the right nigga."

Tiffany shook her head and thought that Lexus wouldn't have hesitated. He would have already left to take care of matters. "Tyrell *is* the right nigga."

"Nah, you kill him and his blood, it'll shut everyone down for at least a year. Five-oh will be all over the place, niggas will start scattering, the paper chase ends."

Tiffany didn't want anything like that to happen, and she understood Blades's point. "What if we made it look like an accident?"

"Look, I ain't saying that it can't be done. It just shouldn't be done. But if it must get done, you need someone who is close to him to do it. Someone who already got access."

Tiffany visited an old friend the next morning. Black was one of her father's old buddies from back in the '70s. Never truly a part of her father's business, he did run a successful numbers game way back. He had been arrested thirty-seven times for everything from rape to murder, and had spent many years in jail. Recently, she heard he had been released from prison, but she stayed clear of him. Her father always mentioned how Black was a liability, to be used only when desperate. Desperate, she was.

"It's Tiffany," she said when she heard someone lift the latch on the peephole.

"Who is it!" he asked in a throaty, raspy voice.

"Tiffany, Shon's daughter."

Black opened the door in his robe, smoking a cigarette. He blew the smoke in the air. "I thought it was your daddy coming back from the dead. You look just like your OG daddy."

Tiffany hesitated about walking in the apartment. It smelled like urine, the kitchen was stacked with dirty plates, and the walls were covered with roaches. "I need to talk to you," she said when she finally walked in.

Black's cigarette hung on the edge of his lips, below pensive eyes.

"I need you to do me a favor."

"Black don't do no more favors." He coughed several times. "I did favors for folks, and see where it landed me?"

Tiffany wiped a roach off her arm. She thought that Black did look bad. His skin was dry and blotchy, and his eyes were reddish. Suddenly she regretted coming to him.

Then Black said, "But I'll listen."

"I need you to take somebody out. He's in New York. He's in the game, and he has to go. His wife and kid, too."

Black smoked his cigarette and looked straight ahead for a few minutes. "I am a fifty-five-year-old man. I don't have it like I used to. I got arthritis. My trigger finger ain't happy no more."

"I got fifty thousand dollars. That's the best I can do," Tiffany said, pulling out wads of cash from her bag.

Black's eyes stayed glued to the money. "They say you can take the thug out of the hood, but you can't take the hood out of the thug." He laughed. "I can use that to get up out of this place."

"But you gotta do this. Can you?"

"What?" Black laughed again. "I've been looking for an ultimate payday. Now, tell me what we talkin' 'bout here. Are we talking assassination, accidental murder, torture—what you need?"

Tiffany grinned. "I just need them dead. Anyhow. Problem is, they ain't together now. So, it may be hard to get them all in the same place. If that's the case, I want Tyrell first. Save Kanika for me." Tiffany slipped him half the cash. "I'll give you the other half when you done."

"Nah, I want fifty thousand dollars to start, and another fifty thousand when I'm done. You talking about a lot of work. Not to mention one of them a baby."

"Fine, a hundred thousand. I just want this done!" Tiffany exploded in frustration. "I don't wanna discuss all the details. Just take care of it."

Black showed off his yellow teeth in a wide grin. "Do you know you making a deal with the devil?"

"I never forget what my daddy told me about you."

"Cool, consider it done," he said, and squashed a roach on the table with his thumb.

Chapter 30

What you smiling about?" Rasheeda asked Tiffany as she walked by her bedroom. "Last I heard, you was shut down."

"Ever heard of the comeback?"

"No, but I've heard of payback. That's what you'll get if you keep fuckin' with Tyrell."

"Whatever, this is back pay. Something completely different. That nigga and Kanika owe me for what they did to my father. I'm just taking back what's rightfully mine."

"So what you smiling about?"

"I found someone who can get me some back pay."

"Who?"

"Black?"

"Black Sam?"

"Yup, I met him the other night, and it's going down. I'm ready for this to be over with. I'm ready to build my shit back in a whole new way," Tiffany said as she put away her 2 and unloaded two 9s on her dresser. She put them all away in a leather case.

"Do you know that man will only bring you more problems?"

"Please, he did this time already. This is gonna be like his last hit."

"That is the same nigga who drowned that family with the babies in that house just a few miles from my own. He cut the man's eyes out, girl!"

"Because that man was behind on some money he owed Black, like two hundred thousand dollars."

"I'm saying, ain't nobody deserve being cut up like that. He's the only black man I know who kill people like that. That's white boy shit."

"That's why I hollered at him. I needed someone who ain't about game playing. I'd take Tyrell's eyes and his balls." Tiffany laughed. "I'll take Kanika's whole head."

Rasheeda turned her nose up at Tiffany. "You know, I liked you because you was a wild young one. Ready to do whatever. But I'm thinking, girl, you are fortified crazy. You done caught the mental on my ass."

Tiffany rolled her neck to the side. "You try seeing your father murdered in front of you in cold blood. You try being left to hold his body and the only other man I ever loved!"

"Don't act like your daddy didn't ask for it," Rasheeda said, shaking her head. "From what I heard, Tyrell and 'em was just defending themselves."

"Fuck it!" Tiffany said, and spun around. "This is what I need to do. You don't have to understand me, but don't judge."

Rasheeda pursed her glossy lips together. She smiled to herself. "Nah, you right. I can't judge. I got my own little secrets and things. But Black is someone I'd never do business with."

"Well, I did. Is there anything else you wanna tell me? Because I am tired. I have a long couple of days ahead of me."

Rasheeda walked in and closed the door behind her. "Actually, there is."

Tiffany looked at her, annoyed.

"Ruby Red is moving in."

"In this house?"

Rasheeda shook her head.

"So what are we playing now? *Three's Company?*" Tiffany scoffed. "I really can't stand that bitch."

"That brings me to my next thing. You should get your own place. We did this thing for a while, and it ain't working for me anymore."

Tiffany's mouth fell open. "You not serious."

"You need your own place. You can leave when the baby is born."

"Hell no! I ain't leaving here. This is my house as well as anybody else's."

"Look, Ruby Red is my woman now, and I ain't about to let you fuck that up like you did Diana."

Tiffany flicked the lights off in the room. "You just wait and see. That Ruby Red bitch is playing you. She is a twenty-two-year-old girl. Why'd she wanna be with your thirty-something ass if it wasn't for money?"

"Kiss my ass, Tiffany," Rasheeda said. She laughed and walked out the room, calling out, "Because you will never kiss it again."

A *few* days later, Ruby Red started moving her things in.

"Put my sofa over there, in that corner," she instructed one of the movers.

Tiffany watched from the top of the stairs as Ruby Red pointed around like she owned everything.

"This place got too much white," Ruby Red said to herself. "Thank God for my green sofa."

"I don't know why Rasheeda would let you bring an old green sofa into her Italian white leather living room," Tiffany said as she walked down.

Ruby Red just smiled. "Don't worry, girl. I know how it is to get booted," she said, and sat on her green sofa to watch the moving men go in and out.

"Whatever. What she did to me, she'll do to you. Ever asked about her last girl, Diana?"

"Why should I? She said the girl split on her, abandoned her. To me, that sounds trifling."

"Oh, and you'd never do that," Tiffany said in a sarcastic tone with her arms folded against her chest.

Ruby Red stayed silent.

"You are a twenty-two-year-old—what the hell can you do for a woman like Rasheeda? You don't even look as good as I do."

"I'll do what you did," Ruby Red said, making tongue motions. Then she laughed.

Tiffany balled her fists up. "That's probably all you fucking good for. Don't think you running shit because you got Rasheeda. She got a lot of bitches. And I don't plan on going anywhere."

"That's up to you," Ruby Red huffed. "But things are going exactly as I planned. I wanted Rasheeda, and I got her. Now, I'm laid up in luxury, getting paid, and I got respect. I didn't only take over Rasheeda's body, but I took over her mind. Once you spit that baby out, we'll be a happy family."

Tiffany tried to contain herself. "I couldn't care two bits about having this chump baby in me. But I will kill myself or this baby before I let you near it!"

"Girl, please. You so dramatic," Ruby Red said, and she lit a cigarette. "You know Rasheeda is giving you thousands for that baby, right?"

Tiffany took a deep breath. "Thousands. How much?"

"I think she mentioned something like six figures. I told her it was too much."

Tiffany couldn't remember anything about Rasheeda paying her for the baby. She had gladly been going to give it up for free. She wondered if the payoff was supposed to be a surprise. "Rasheeda is gonna pay me. Well, I want that money before I leave."

"Talk to Rasheeda," Ruby Red said, dismissing her with her hand. "It looks like you gonna need it with your little business being shut down. You are so over, girl." Ruby Red busted out in a loud laugh.

*T*iffany remained in her bedroom for the rest of the night as she listened to Ruby Red's laughter coming from Rasheeda's bedroom. She cringed at the moans that came much later. She had a small sack of white powder under her bed. She emptied it on her nightstand and inhaled.

Chapter 31

Are you sure this is safe?" Sheila asked Kanika as they headed out to Tiffany's new spot in Queens.

"I'm not sure. But I need to find that bitch Tiffany. I know she's in New York. If we can find some of her people on the corner, we can ask. You got your piece on you?"

"Of course," Sheila said, feeling the cold metal against her hip. "None of them niggas better fuck with you, or else I'm capping them first, asking questions later."

Kanika smiled as she steered the car into an empty lot. The desolate area was treeless and littered with garbage. Tall, lanky teens stood on the corners, holding up their posts. There was one who looked like he was the lookout as he made his rounds back and forth on the block.

"We need to talk to *him*," Kanika said, pointing to the dude who stood solo against the wall. He was shorter than the others, but appeared to be the one they listened to.

Kanika wasn't sure how she'd play her angle, but she definitely didn't want to give away who she really was. They decided that Sheila would do all the talking.

They walked slowly in front of the guy while Sheila dropped

her keys at his feet. He bent down to pick them up and handed them to her.

"Oh, thank you," she said in a flirtatious tone. "Have we you seen you before?"

"Nah," said the guy as he eyed Kanika. He was feeling both of them. "I ain't never seen you chicks around here before."

"What's your name?" Sheila asked as she put out her hand. "I'm Sheila."

He looked at her hand like it was a foreign object. He wasn't used to that. He nodded his head. "I'm Ras."

"Is it for the dreads in your hair?" Sheila smiled.

"Yeah, something like that," Ras said, licking his lips. He checked Kanika out again. "You look mad familiar," he told her.

Kanika looked behind her like he was talking to someone else. "Me? I hardly come out here. You ain't never seen me before."

"What's your name?" he asked.

"Keisha." Kanika hoped she sounded convincing.

Ras grunted as he put his attention back on Sheila. "So what you ladies getting into today? Ya don't look like crackheads." He laughed.

"We looking for an old friend. Maybe you heard of her. Tiffany?"

Ras narrowed his eyes, pretending concentration. "Nah, I don't know her."

"She's a little round thing. From VA?"

"Nah, I don't," Ras said again.

But Kanika could tell from his eyes that he was lying.

"If we wanted to get down, make some money, who we talk to?"

"You talk to me," Ras said, pulling out a wad of cash. "But y'all don't look like you push rocks. You five-oh?"

"Hell no!" Sheila said, and she and Kanika laughed. "We was about to ask you that."

Ras laughed nervously, too. "Nah, just asking because things been hot lately. We gotta watch our backs." Ras turned to Kanika, but she looked away.

"But for real, we wanna get down. What we gotta do?" Sheila asked with more persistence.

"Well, you ready to start today?"

"Maybe, but I wanna speak to the head person in charge. I heard some VA folks run this shit."

"Yeah, and?"

"Can we make real paper or what?"

Ras seemed to relax a bit. "To be honest, things are mad slow. It was much better when Tyrell, that dude from Brooklyn, had his peeps around here. I used to roll with them, but then niggas said I could make more money on this new spot. But man, how rich can you get selling five-dollar bags a few times a day? Them heads is going someplace else for their hit. They getting it from Tyrell." Ras flashed his eyes to Kanika. "Now, I think I know you."

Kanika eased her hand on her hips. Sheila peeped her move.

"Ain't you his wife? What you doin' up here?" Ras asked, his nose flaring. He pushed Kanika against the wall.

"Don't fucking touch me, nigga," Kanika said, pushing back.

Sheila grabbed him in a choke hold, but Ras flipped around and mushed Sheila in her face.

That was when Kanika pulled out her heat and capped him three times in the back. Ras tumbled to the ground. She helped Sheila up from the ground, and then they ran to their car. Before they knew it, they were speeding down Farmer's Boulevard on a high she hadn't experienced in years.

Kanika spent the night at Sheila's. Her mouth wasn't badly

busted. She had a small splinter on top of her lip. They both agreed that they wouldn't mention the incident to Sheila's husband, Big Gee.

In the morning, Kanika arrived at the spa with Sheila. The news had traveled faster than she expected.

"Girl, did you hear what happened in Jamaica last night?" Denise said to Kanika. She talked with the curling iron in her hand.

"What happened?" Kanika asked, acting surprised.

"Somebody went up there and blasted Ras. Ras is supposed to be one of the niggas who helped those VA peeps take over Tyrell's spot. I heard niggas scattered after that. It's mad quiet up there now."

Kanika and Sheila smiled at each other.

"So what that mean?" Sheila asked Denise.

"It means niggas is going someplace else. They ain't trying to hang around there."

"It also means Tyrell can take over that spot again," Kanika said quietly. "The hold Tiffany and her little crew had was weak. If it take one nigga going down to shut it down, it didn't deserve to be in place from the start."

"Exactly," Sheila chimed in.

Denise looked at Kanika and Sheila suspiciously, but Kanika went about her business, scanning the appointment sheet for the morning and making sure the place looked spic and span for opening in about twenty minutes. She heard Tyrell's voice outside in the front. He was talking to a few dudes from the barbershop. He didn't get out his car, but drove off.

"That was Tyrell, girl. You wasn't gonna say something?" Sheila whispered in her ear.

"I ain't got shit to say to him."

"But we almost got fucked up last night, looking after his own business."

"It's my business, too, Sheila. I was protecting my assets. Because the less Tyrell owns, the less that means for all of us. Let him think one of his boys did it," she said, as she high-heeled her way to the mirror. She combed her long tresses and tried to contain her heartbeat. She missed Tyrell, but she knew she couldn't stand looking at him yet.

Denise stood next to her. "I guess he's back in business up there."

"Good for him."

Denise looked at Kanika in the mirror. "Did you do anything?"

"Never," Kanika said, applying a thick coat of mascara.

"For real?"

"Let me just say this: I will do whatever I have to to protect what's mine."

Denise simply nodded and walked away.

Kanika knew she had more work ahead of her. Tiffany was still out there, and she wasn't going to rest. In fact, she thought, Ras was just a practice.

A*re you* okay?" asked Ms. Smith when Kanika returned. She was sitting by the window with a distressed look on her face when Kanika walked in.

Kanika felt guilty when she realized how upset Ms. Smith was. "I'm sorry I didn't call. It was too late. I really didn't expect to stay in New York. How's Little T?"

"He's fine. Slept like an angel. But dear, you could've at least called. Just one phone call," Ms. Smith said, wringing her hands together.

Kanika sat down slowly on the chair and felt like she was six-
teen all over again. She hadn't expected Ms. Smith to react like
this. Maybe her stay was taking its toll on Ms. Smith. "Since my
mother passed, I've never really had anyone to answer to. I'm sorry
again for not calling, and maybe that's why it slipped my mind.
But I don't want to cause you any stress, Ms. Smith. I'm sure you've
had enough of that in your life."

Ms. Smith sat down on a burgundy Victorian armchair. "I
sure have. That's why I can tell you are going through lots right
now. I also feel something awful happened last night. I had a
dream about you running."

Kanika darted her eyes from the floor to the ceiling. She
couldn't look at Ms. Smith. She had forgotten that older folks had
an intuitive sense, but she couldn't admit the truth. "No, really,
Ms. Smith, I was with a girlfriend of mine and we got carried
away. We hung out for me to destress a little," Kanika said.

"Did you see Tyrell?" Ms. Smith asked.

That stopped Kanika dead in her tracks. "No, I didn't."

"Why not?"

"Because I wanted to destress," Kanika said, turning around.
"I didn't want to argue with him. Let's just say I handled my business, but not with him."

"I'm gonna be frank with you," Ms. Smith said in a low, warm
voice. "I'm not comfortable anymore keeping you from your husband. If you are really serious about leaving him, you can file a
separation and stay here until you find a place. If not, you need to
go back home."

Kanika sat back down. "Are you kicking me out?" she asked
with a crooked smile.

"Not at all. But I want you to understand your responsibility as
a wife. You have to work this out with Tyrell. I'm sure you didn't
see your mama run out every time something bad happened?"

"My mama never went through anything like this."

"How do you know?"

Kanika didn't know. Her mother told her many things, but certainly not everything.

Ms. Smith cleared her throat. "Child, you still love that man, and he loves and adores you. You're like his little princess. He'd do anything for you. People make mistakes—"

"This is a big one."

"I still think you need to investigate—"

"I did try to find Tiffany. I want to handle this woman-to-woman with her. At least."

Ms. Smith grinned. "That's exactly right. Once you do that, then you can make your decision. But at some point, you have to decide whether you want to fight or flight."

Chapter 32

You got all the information you need, right?" Tiffany asked as she sat on the bed in a motel room in Times Square with only one lamp and a shared bathroom.

Tiffany had arrived in New York with Black just before dawn on a Monday morning.

"Of course. I'm a pro, baby."

"Did you find out where he works?"

"I know everything about the nigga, from where he shits to the length of the hairs on his dick." He laughed.

"That's a little too much info."

"Well, when you in jail for as long as I've been, you get to know men in a whole different kind of way," Black said.

Tiffany didn't want to hear any more. "Where are you gonna do it at?"

Black wiped down his guns and arranged his armor on the bed. "I figured I'd catch him at night. Probably at the crib."

"They got tight security in the building. I think it's best when he leaves the building. Like right outside," Tiffany said, getting excited.

Black glared at her. "Let me handle this. Night or day, the

nigga is going down. I usually don't decide these types of things so early, anyway."

"It's two days away. And don't forget I need his wife dead, too."

"What about the baby?"

"The baby is all the way Upstate," Tiffany said, holding her cramping belly. "Just focus on Tyrell and Kanika. It's easy and quick. And a little baby that's left ain't gonna trouble nobody."

"Cool," Black said with a mischievous grin. "Would you like to do the honors?" He handed her a Glock and bullets.

Tiffany loaded the barrel. She relished every click. She gave it back to him.

"Not bad, see somebody taught you well. Now, what about my transportation back to VA?"

"Here," Tiffany said, handing him keys to a car. "You have to drive back."

"Hell no," Black said. "I drive back, and niggas stop me at a checkpoint somewhere in D.C. I ain't going back to jail. Fuck that!"

Tiffany flinched at the anger in his voice. "Fine, fine. I will get you a train ticket."

"No, bitch, I wanna plane. First class. I wanna be in Virginia no more than two hours from when I do my shit. From there, I got other plans."

Tiffany rolled her eyes in annoyance because now she had to find a plane ticket in little time. Her stomach ached, her head hurt, and she needed relief. "I'll get you what you want, as long as you do what I want, the way I want it," Tiffany said, and pointed to her temple.

A *few* hours later, Tiffany had managed to get a ticket for Black. When she got back to Misa's apartment, she had an intense urge to use the bathroom. She was only three months pregnant, and had dealt with constipation, but at this moment she was feeling something new.

Tiffany stood over the toilet spitting up and feeling faint. When she finally sat down, she felt her stomach cramp even more. She bent over the toilet in heart-wrenching pain. She put her hand between her legs, looked at it, and noticed blood. She yelled. Inside the toilet were huge specks of blood clots and excrement. She'd had a miscarriage. Tiffany felt the room spin, and she collapsed on the floor with blood still trickling between her thighs. The toilet was covered in blood. She reached over and flushed it. She wailed in pain some more and laid her back on the cold floor. After some time, she stood up, cleaned up, and put it behind her. She knew this could mess up her plans with Tyrell, but if she kept wearing big clothes, she thought she could get away with the "pregnancy" for a few more months. A part her was relieved, but then she thought about Rasheeda, and made a phone call.

"Rasheeda?"

"It's late," Rasheeda mumbled into the phone. "I was asleep."

"I know, but I gotta talk to you," Tiffany said, hoping she could get some sympathy from Rasheeda.

"What happened this time?" Rasheeda asked sarcastically.

"I'm in New York, and I wasn't feeling too good—"

"Oh, I wanted to tell you before you left that I had a talk with Ruby Red. I wanna give you some money for the baby. How's two hundred and fifty thousand?"

"To have the baby?"

"Yes, stupid."

Tiffany couldn't believe her luck. Ruby Red, she thought, may have had lots of influence in making Rasheeda pay her. She liked that.

"So?" Rasheeda asked.

"Since I didn't want this baby in the first place, how's five hundred thousand dollars?"

"Three hundred and fifty thousand, and that's my final," Rasheeda said. "And a crack pipe," she joked.

Tiffany rolled her eyes at her little dis. "I'll think about it." Tiffany knew that she'd take it in a heartbeat. She planned to hide what happened from everyone.

"You can use the money to get your own place, too," Rasheeda said. "When you have the baby, I want you out."

"I want the money before I have the baby," Tiffany said. "I need to have money if I have to get a place. Or else I'm gonna be staying with you for as long as it takes."

Rasheeda thought for a few seconds. "Well, that is true. I'll give it to you when you come back. But Tiffany, if I find out that you trying to play me, I will burn your skin down to the fat meat."

Tiffany awoke to Misa standing over her head. "My bathroom is a fucking mess. Where'd the blood come from? You're not having your period anymore, are you?"

Tiffany wet her eyes with saliva and rolled over to look at Misa. "I had a miscarriage."

Misa knelt down by the bed and felt Tiffany's head for a fever. The lines grew on the side of her mouth. "You need to be in a hospital."

"I went, but they said I was fine," Tiffany said, in a phony sad voice. She was surprised Misa even cared, considering what Tiffany had done with her man. A part of her felt good that she was able to intimidate Misa and keep her from even trying to ask about it. "I was alone."

"Girl, I am so sorry. I feel so bad I wasn't here, and me a nurse. What hospital did you go to? Brookdale?"

"Yeah." Tiffany put on her puppy-dog eyes. "I was so scared."

Misa hugged Tiffany. "You should've called me."

"Even after what I did?"

"It doesn't matter," Misa said, shrugging her shoulders. "He was no good, anyway."

But Tiffany could see the fear in Misa's eyes. Misa didn't want to start anything. Tiffany held in her smile. "I didn't wanna bother you," Tiffany said.

"Are you sure you okay?"

Tiffany nodded. "I'm just hungry."

Misa hopped up. "Don't you worry. Just lay down and I'll cook you something. You like eggs and bacon?"

Tiffany wiped fake tears from her eyes. "Sunny side up."

Misa smiled and walked off to the kitchen. In minutes, Tiffany heard her banging away at pots and pans in the kitchen. Soon the crackling of bacon sounded off, and the delicious smell filled the apartment.

She flipped the TV on and stretched her legs out in the bed in a comfortable position. It wasn't long before Misa arrived with a tray of bacon, eggs, toast, and orange juice. "This should have you feeling a lot better."

Tiffany moved slowly. She was still in pain.

Misa fed her some of the eggs. "Are they good?"

"Very good," Tiffany said, as she started to feed herself. "Thanks."

Misa peered into her eyes. "You need to stay in bed today. I'll be around if you need anything. What do you like for dinner?"

"Meat loaf and sweet potatoes."

"Okay, I can do that. You really don't need to be doing much."

"I know, because shit is about to get crazy out there again," she hinted to Misa.

"What's going on?"

"Tyrell may be looking at his last days," Tiffany said, and munched on the toast. "But you didn't hear it from me."

"Tyrell? He's iron-clad. If he hasn't been taken out by now, nobody has the guts to."

"We'll see about that," Tiffany said.

Chapter 33

Two weeks later, Kanika spent the afternoon in Manhattan filing separation papers from Tyrell. She thought that no explanation could make her feel at peace with the fact that he even touched Tiffany. She couldn't decide what hurt her heart more—the loathing she had for Tiffany or Tyrell's betrayal. She knew once he got the papers he would be crushed. She already was.

"All right, your husband should have these papers in just a few days. Do you need anything else?" asked Mr. Stein, her lawyer, as he touched his clean-shaven chin.

"Not right now. I just need this all to sink in."

"You're taking the right steps. I hate it when people just want to divorce. Separation gives you that time apart to make rational decisions."

She was waiting for that feeling of relief and excitement to hit her, but it never did. "Right, thank you," Kanika said, and left the office, walking onto the sunny New York City streets.

She stopped by a pizza shop and picked up a slice. On her way to the parking lot, a voice called out to her. She spun around, and a very short woman with cropped red hair, high heels, and a mink jacket—even though it was a warm September day—approached her.

"Is you Kanika? Waleema little girl?" asked the woman.

Kanika smiled. "Depends who's asking?" She noticed the lady's tiny dark keloids under her eyes. The woman looked familiar, but Tiffany couldn't place her.

"This is Mabel. One of the bartenders at your mama club. 'Member me?" Mabel flashed her signature gold-toothed grin.

"Yes, yes, I remember," Kanika said, throwing her arms around her. "Wow, it's been a while."

She grabbed Kanika's left hand. "You married Tyrell?"

Kanika nodded.

"What a blessing! Amen. I knew you two were born for each other. I had moved out of Brooklyn. I work at a club up in Harlem now."

"Is that where you're headed?"

"Yeah. I need to get to work."

"Let me drop you off," Kanika offered.

Mabel grinned again. "You are just as gracious as your mama. Thank you, darling," Mabel said, as she and Kanika walked up the block to the parking lot.

When the attendant pulled out Tiffany's shiny black Range Rover, she noticed Mabel's eyes get wide.

"Now, that's a car!" Mabel laughed.

Kanika did, too, at Mabel's simple way of putting things. They hopped in her ride, and Mabel rambled on about her new job.

"Well, Mabel, I am really happy that you are keeping your head up. What happened was a blow to all of you," Kanika said as they sped up the West Side Highway.

"Especially you. I mean, you were a diamond in your mama's eyes. Tony loved you. You were luckier than all them other kids on the block."

Kanika frowned. "At least their parents are still alive."

There were a few minutes of silence until Mabel said, "How's Tyrell?"

"He's all right, but we're not together right now."

"Ain't you two married?"

"Yeah, but we are taking some time apart."

"You kids these days are so smart. Women like your mama and me, we dealt with so much shit from men. We stayed there mostly because we didn't have a place to go."

Kanika looked over at Mabel, who seemed upset. "You know, I think my mama was one of those lucky women who had a good man. My mama and Tony were usually happy."

"Tony?" Mabel let out a choppy laugh. "He had his ways."

"What you mean?" Kanika asked. Mabel had worked at the club since its opening, and she'd known Waleema for more than half her life.

"No offense, but Tony had his share of women. Your mama dealt with a lot."

"I know they had their fights—"

"Did you know he had another family?"

Kanika swerved the car to avoid hitting the one in front of her. "Are we talking about the same Tony?"

"Yes. He had a Spanish chick up in the Bronx named Suzette. They had a little boy together. When he died, she moved back to Puerto Rico. One of those."

"And her son?"

"He went, too. You never knew?"

"No." Kanika tried to catch her breath. She didn't remember anything about that. Her mother and Tony acted like she was the only one in their world.

"Just trying to tell you, girl, I know the kind of lives these men like Tony and Tyrell live. You are a smart young girl. Get out while you can," Mabel said, looking at her with a dead serious expression.

Kanika felt frightened. She knew that it was not the kind of married life she wanted with Tyrell—a life of silence and denial.

*B*efore she headed back Upstate, Kanika stopped by the spa. She wanted to check in on her girls and make sure things were in order.

When she arrived, everyone had headed home for the evening, except for Sheila, who was closing up.

"How was today?" Sheila asked as she swept the floor.

Kanika sat down on one of the spa chairs. "It went better than I thought. When I left the office, I wasn't that sure, but then I saw an old friend of my mom's who told me I was doing the right thing."

"Who was that?"

"This lady Mabel. Told me about some things my mom had to deal with. I knew I couldn't do that, and I think that is where Tyrell and I were headed."

Sheila shook her head. "One thing you have that a lot of us around here don't is smarts. If it wasn't for the game, I know you'd be a doctor or something. You don't need a man," Sheila said.

"You're wrong, Sheila. I do. I just need the right man who will respect and love me. I ain't sitting down while he does what he wants."

"But another thing." Sheila stopped sweeping. "I never seen a man love a woman like Tyrell loves you."

Kanika looked to the ground. "What about Big Gee?"

"Please, we don't even sleep in the same bed anymore. We

can't stand each other, but I deal with it. I could only dream of what it's like to have him hold me, make love to me, tell me how good I look and feel. Buy me things. You have all that."

"And Tyrell fucked it up," Kanika said, looking at herself in the mirror. "I still got my looks, and he's not taking away my best years." Kanika laughed a little, but her heart was heavy. She wanted Tyrell to come through those doors and whisk her away, but she couldn't let that happen, even if he did.

Sheila attended to a call on her cell while Kanika read over the books for the money they'd made that day. They had raked in almost five thousand dollars. It was no surprise—the spa pulled in nearly that much every day. She thought that maybe if she spent more time there, it could double and she had just the ideas to do that.

"What's wrong with you?" Kanika asked when she saw the grimace on Sheila's face.

"I just heard that some dude is out there about to kill Tyrell. Tonight."

"Who told you that?"

"Who else? Big Gee. He has some people in VA. It could be a rumor, but don't take any chances."

Kanika looked at Sheila sideways. "Girl, you are crazy. Anyway—"

"I'm serious!" Sheila said, and shook Kanika. "Somebody is gonna kill Tyrell."

Kanika stared into Sheila's long face, which was filled with pain. She grabbed her phone and bag and raced to the door.

"Where are you going?" Sheila said, rushing behind her.

"To find Tyrell," Kanika cried. "I gotta find him—"

"Girl, you can't! You don't want to get caught in this—" Sheila said, blocking the door.

"Get off me, Sheila," Kanika said as she pushed Sheila out the way, jumped in her truck, and dialed Tyrell.

She couldn't reach him. She dialed Big Gee. Nothing.

She drove through the traffic-congested streets. Her tears clouded her vision and her heart beat against her chest like a drum. She thought she'd go to the Brooklyn office, but then something told her to go up to the Manhattan apartment. She prayed to God she wouldn't get there too late.

Chapter 34

Tyrell turned the key to his apartment, walked in, and expected Kanika to be at the door like every evening. He wanted her back more than anything. He hoped she could see that everything he was doing was for her.

Tiffany was shut down. That meant she'd be too preoccupied with her own destruction to go after somebody else's. He wanted to get Tiffany off their backs for good.

He showered and readied for bed, and then slept on his side. Kanika's side was still untouched and had strands of her hair on the pillow. He hadn't changed the sheets since she left. He was losing himself. Sometimes he'd smell the pillow just to be near her. He lay on his back and thought about everything that had gone wrong. Maybe he did sleep with Tiffany, he thought to himself. Maybe she was having his baby. For the life of him, he couldn't remember enough to say for sure that he hadn't. That was why he hated alcohol, because any minute he had no control over was a minute too long. He wondered what Kanika was doing tonight, and who she was with. There was no doubt in his mind that mad brothas were checking for her. He just didn't want to know who they were.

He closed his eyes and then swore he heard the latch on the apartment door open. He opened his eyes, but heard nothing now. He tried to sleep, but something was off. When he got up to check the door, it was locked, but the foyer light was on. He was sure he had turned it off. He went to the kitchen to pour himself a glass of water, then back to bed. He dialed Kanika's phone. She didn't answer, but he left a message.

"Just calling to see if you can't sleep like me. Don't know where you at now at almost midnight, but I want you to call me when you get in. I miss you. I love you. One," he said, and hung up. He glanced at his watch and started to get a little heated. Where the hell could she be? He dialed her number again, but got nothing. About an hour later, he heard the sound of light footsteps. The faucet in the kitchen was turned on, and he listened as the water ran. He flashed his eyes open and smiled. Kanika was back home. He listened carefully again. The footsteps sounded light and careful, just like hers.

"Kanika," Tyrell called out. As soon as he heard nothing back, he knew he'd made a bad mistake. He grabbed his gun from under the pillow. He hopped out of the bed and cocked his gun as he trod slowly out of the room. "Muthafucka, it's just me and you. Come get me, nigga."

Tyrell wasn't sure who he was talking to, but he felt a dark presence. He could even hear a man breathing. He turned on the lights in the apartment and tried to follow the sound of the breath.

"Come out, nigga!" Tyrell gripped his gun, about to set it off on anything. He didn't even feel his heart beat, as if he knew he was dead already. He knew he was being watched. Then he saw a red dot on his chest. When he pulled the clip, a bullet dived into him at the exact point of the red dot. He dragged his bloody torso to the doorway as the red dot followed his every move. He managed to stand up until a barrage of bullets penetrated his body.

The sheer force and pain traveled down his body as he let out his final round to whoever. "Kanika," he whispered, and finally collapsed facedown on the floor, never seeing a soul.

About an hour later, Kanika finally made it home to chaos. Several cop cars and officers were in front of her building.

"Excuse me, excuse me," Kanika said, panicked, as she pushed through the crowd standing outside and ran inside the building.

"What happened?" she asked a new security guard at the desk.

"Somebody was shot in apartment 22E."

"What!" Kanika shouted, and ran to the elevator. She banged on the elevator door as it slowly came down. Her eyes ran as she cried uncontrollably. Several officers came out of the elevator when it arrived.

"Oh my God, my husband, we live in 22E," she said to one of them.

"Are you Kanika?" asked the tall dark-haired one.

"Yes, where is he?"

The officers looked at each other. Then the same one said, "He was taken away by ambulance, unconscious. That's all we know now. We just came from gathering some evidence."

Kanika nearly fainted, and one of the officers grabbed her arm. "You have to find who did this!" she cried.

"All we know is whoever did is an expert. They came through the roof."

"Can I go up?" Kanika asked.

The officers nodded, and Kanika got on the elevator. She didn't believe them. Her Tyrell couldn't be shot, couldn't be unconscious. *No, no, no.* She had to see it for herself. *He'll be right upstairs,* she thought. They had the wrong person.

Kanika walked into her yellow-taped apartment as a few other officers made their way out. The walls were stained with blood. Kanika ran her hands along the wall and her fingers dripped with the blood. No one seemed to notice her; they all knew she must be the wife.

"Can we ask you a few questions?" asked an officer.

"No!" Kanika yelled. Her body shivered as she felt Tyrell's presence. He was still there with her. She wanted to stay in the apartment and breathe him in. She couldn't go to the hospital, not yet.

Against the orders of the investigators and the officers who escorted her away, Kanika snuck back to the quiet, dark crime scene. She wanted whoever had done this to Tyrell to do it to her, too. Then she thought of Little T.

At last she was ready. Tyrell wasn't coming back home, she thought. The last thing she wanted to do was see his bullet-ridden body in the hospital, but she knew what she had to.

"Going somewhere?" she heard a girl's voice in the dark.

She flicked on the lights, and there she was standing face-to-face with Tiffany.

"You did this," Kanika said with a stone face. "Why didn't you just come get me!"

"I am, bitch," Tiffany said, as she stepped closer. "But I wanted to get who you loved the most."

"You already destroyed me when you fucked Tyrell. Wasn't that good enough!"

Tiffany laughed. "No, he's not dead yet."

Kanika pulled out her heat and aimed it at Tiffany's head. "You making this so easy for me, Tiffany."

"You gonna kill Tyrell's baby?"

Kanika cringed, but she kept the gun steady. She didn't know what she was ready to do. But all her tears were gone. She was ready to fight.

"What if I told you that this baby isn't Tyrell's and I didn't fuck him," Tiffany said, not caring anymore. She knew she was a dead woman.

Kanika raised her aim a little higher. "What?"

"That's right, I lied." Tiffany grinned. "Broke y'all up, and I did it all because I could!" She charged at Kanika and wrestled her for the gun.

Kanika and Tiffany fell to the ground as they tussled. The gun jumped out of Kanika's hand, but she grabbed it back in time. Tiffany jumped on Kanika's back and grabbed the gun, too, but as Kanika turned around, it went off in her half sister's face. As brain matter flew everywhere, Tiffany fell back onto the floor and exhaled for the final time.

Chapter 35

Ma'am, we may call you to ask further questions, but this does look like self-defense," said a police officer who had arrived on the scene. Kanika couldn't bear to abandon Tiffany's body, like someone had Tyrell's.

"I told you many times already, this woman was gonna kill me if I didn't. I believe this woman also had something to do with my husband being shot." Kanika put her hand on her chest. "Can I go now?"

The police officer nodded as the paramedics took Tiffany's covered body out the door. Kanika quickly left the building. Her body felt cold and deadened. It was like the life had been sucked out of her. She wanted desperately to be in Tyrell's arms, but silently thanked God she had waited. She was also relieved that Tiffany was gone for good.

Kanika's bloodstained hands gripped the wheel of her truck as she drove to St. Luke's Hospital. She told herself she didn't mean to kill Tiffany, but someone was going to die eventually. She hoped it wasn't Tyrell.

At the hospital, Tyrell was connected to a heart monitor and wrapped in bandages.

"How is he?" Kanika asked the doctor who walked in. "Is he gonna die?"

The doctor shook his head. "He's hurt badly. He has a fractured rib cage, and a bullet is lodged in his liver. It also looks like he hit his head exceptionally hard when he fell. He has some brain hemorrhage. We want to watch him for a few days. These forty-eight hours are the most crucial, but he has a good chance of making it."

Kanika sat alongside the bed next to his still body. She kissed his forehead several times, then his dry, cracked lips. His mouth parted slightly when he saw her. But he couldn't speak.

"I should've listened to you," Kanika whispered in his ear. "I'm sorry."

Tyrell turned his head slowly toward her.

"The bitch is dead."

A weak smile appeared across Tyrell's lips.

"We're gonna go far away from here, Tyrell. I can't risk almost losing you again. We gotta go somewhere and start over—," she pleaded with him.

Tyrell took her hand with a strength she didn't think he'd have in him. "We can go anywhere as long as we stay a family," he managed to say.

"Will you promise you'll never leave me?" she asked him.

"You can leave me a thousand times, but I'll be with you for life," he said, and closed his eyes.